Christmas

In

Silver Bell Falls

By

Samantha

Chase

To My Favorite Romance Chasers

I cannot thank you enough for the love and support you show me on a daily basis. You are the reason I do what I do and why I love it so much.

Your love and friendship is a blessing to me and I want you all to know how amazing you are.

This book is for you.

Chapter One

There was nothing quite like coming home at the end of a long day: kicking off your shoes…having a little something to eat while watching TV…and most importantly, not having to hear any more Christmas music!

Melanie Harper was certain she wasn't the only one who felt that way. It was early November and the holiday season was just getting under way.

"More like under my skin," she murmured as she walked into her kitchen and poured herself a glass of wine. Taking her glass, she went back to her living room and sat down on the couch.

It had been a long day. A long week. Hell, if she were being honest, it had been a long three months. With deadlines approaching, her editor was getting more and more snarky while Melanie was getting more and more discouraged.

Writer's block.

In her ten years of writing, she'd never once suffered from it, but for some reason the words refused to come.

"Figures," she said with disgust and turned on the TV. Flipping through the channels, it was all the same thing—Christmas specials, Christmas movies and holiday-themed shows. Unable to stand it, she turned it off and sighed.

It was always like this. Christmas. The holidays.
Every year, if something bad was going to happen, it
happened around Christmas.

Not that it had been that way her entire life,
but…she stopped and paused. No, scratch that. It
had been like that her entire life. Her earliest memory
was of the Christmas when she was five. That was
the year her mother left. Her father had been too
distraught to celebrate that year so she spent the day
watching him drink and cry.

There had been a glimmer of hope for the next
year—her dad promised her it would be better. The
flu had both of them fighting for the bathroom the
entire day. And after that, it was all one big, giant
blur of suckiness. Between financial struggles and
family issues—and that one year where they had
gotten robbed the day before Christmas—Melanie
had come to see the months of November and
December as nothing but a big nuisance. Eventually
they stopped even attempting to celebrate.

And now she'd be able to add "getting cut by her
publisher because of writer's block" to the Christmas
resume of doom.

The name almost made her chuckle.

It would have been easy to sit there and wax
unpoetic about how much she hated this time of the
year, but a knock at the door saved her. Placing her
wine glass down, she padded to the front door and
pulled it open.

"Hey! There's my girl!"

Melanie smiled as her dad wrapped her in his embrace. "Hey, Dad." She hugged him back and then stepped aside so he could come in. "What's going on? I thought we were getting together on Saturday for dinner."

John Harper smiled at his only child as he took off his coat. "Is this a bad time?"

She shook her head. "No, not at all. I just wasn't expecting you. Have you eaten dinner yet?"

He chuckled softly. "It's almost eight, Mel. Of course I have." He studied her for a minute. "Don't tell me you haven't."

She shrugged. "It was a long day and I sort of lost my appetite."

"Uh-oh. What happened?"

Melanie led him to the living room and sat down on the couch again. "My deadline will be here at the end of December and I haven't written a thing."

"Okay," he said slowly. "So…can't they extend your deadline?"

She shook her head. "They've extended it three times already."

"Hmm…so what's the problem with the story? Why are you having such a hard time with it? That's not like you."

She sighed again. "They're pretty much demanding a Christmas story."

"Oh."

She didn't even need to look at him to know his expression was just as pinched as hers at the topic. "Yeah…oh."

"Did you try explaining…?"

Nodding, she sat up and reached for her glass of wine. "Every time I talk to them. They don't get it and they don't care. Basically their attitude is that I'm a fiction writer and I should be able to use my imagination to concoct this Christmas story without having to draw on personal experience."

"Maybe they don't realize just how much you dislike the holiday."

"Dislike is too mild of a word," she said flatly. Taking a long drink, she put her glass down and looked at him. "I don't even want to talk about it. The meeting with my editor and agent went on and on and on today so my brain is pretty fried. The only thing to come out of it is yet another crappy reinforcement of the holiday."

"Oh, dear…"

Melanie's eyes narrowed. "What? What's wrong?"

"I guess maybe I should have called first because…" He stopped. "You know what? Never mind. We'll talk on Saturday." He stood quickly and walked back toward the foyer.

"Oh, no," she said as she went after him. "You can't come here and say something like that and then leave! Come on. What's going on?"

John sighed and reached for her hand. "Your grandmother died."

Melanie simply stared at him for a minute. "Oh…okay. Wow. Um…when?"

"A month ago."

Her eyes went wide. "And you're just telling me now?"

Slowly, he led her back to the couch. "Mel, seriously? Your grandmother hasn't spoken to me in over twenty-five years. I'm surprised I was notified."

"I guess," she sighed. Then she looked at him. "Are you okay?"

He shrugged. "I'm not sure. I always thought when the time came that it wouldn't mean anything. After all, she kind of died to me all those years ago. But now? Now that I know she's really gone?" His voice choked with emotion. "It all suddenly seems so stupid, so wrong. I mean, how could I have let all those years go by without trying to make things right?"

Squeezing his hand, Melanie reached over and hugged him. "It's not like you never tried, Dad. Grandma was pretty stubborn. You can't sit here and take all the blame."

When she released him, she saw him wipe away a stray tear. "In my mind, I guess I always thought there would be time. Time to make amends and…"

"I know," she said softly. "And I'm sorry. I really am."

"You probably don't even remember her. You were so little when it all happened."

It was the truth, sort of. Melanie had some memories of her grandmother and none of them were of the warm and fuzzy variety. Unfortunately, now wasn't the time to mention it. "So who contacted you?"

"Her attorney. He actually called last night and met me in person today."

"Well that was nice of him. I guess."

"He had some papers for me. For us."

Melanie looked at him oddly. "What kind of papers?"

"She um…she left some things to us in her will."

Her eyes went wide again. "Seriously? The woman didn't talk to either of us all these years and she actually put us in her will? Is it bad stuff?"

John chuckled. "What do you mean by bad stuff?"

"You know…like she has a really old house and she was a hoarder and we're supposed to clean it out.

Or she has some sort of vicious pet we're supposed to take care of. That kind of thing."

John laughed even harder. "Sometimes your imagination really is wild; you know that, right?" he teased.

Melanie couldn't help but laugh with him. "What? It's true! Things like that happen all the time!"

"Mel, it doesn't," he said, wiping the tears of mirth from his eyes. "And for your information, there was no hoarding, no vicious pets…"

"Did she collect dead animals or something?"

He laughed again. "No. Nothing like that."

Relaxing back on the couch, she looked at her father. "Okay. Lay it on me then. What could she possibly have put in her will for the two of us?"

John took a steadying breath. "She left me my father's coin collection."

That actually made Melanie smile. "I know how much you used to talk about it." She nodded with approval. "That's a good gift to get."

He nodded. "She'd kept it all these years. Then there's some family photos, things from my childhood that she had saved, that sort of thing."

"So no money," Melanie said because she already knew the answer.

John shook his head. "And it's fine with me. I don't think I would have felt comfortable with it. All those years ago, it would have meant the world to me to have a little help so you and I didn't have to struggle so much. But we're good now and I don't really need or want it."

"Who'd she leave it to? Her cat? Some snooty museum?"

"Museums aren't snooty," he said lightly.

"Anyway," she prompted. "So who'd she leave her fortune to?"

With a sigh he took one of her hands in his. "She left the bulk of her estate to the local hospice care center."

"Oh…well…that was nice of her," Melanie said. "I guess she wasn't entirely hateful."

"No, she wasn't," John said softly. "And she did leave you something."

The statement wasn't a surprise since he'd mentioned it earlier, but Melanie figured he'd tell her when he was ready.

"When the attorney told me about it," he began, "I was a little surprised. I had no idea she still had it."

Curiosity piqued, she asked, "Had what?"

"The cabin."

Okay, *that* was a surprise, she thought. "Grandma had a cabin? Where?"

"Up north. Practically on the border of Canada."

"Seriously? Why on earth would she have a cabin there?"

A small smile played across John's face. "Believe it or not, there was a time when your grandmother wasn't quite so…hard. She loved the winters and loved all of the outdoor activities you could do in the snow. She skied, went sleigh riding and…get this…she loved Christmas."

Pulling her hand from his, Melanie stood with a snort of disgust. "That's ironic. The woman went out of her way to ruin so many of our Christmases and now you're telling me she used to love them? So…so…what? She started hating them after I came along? That would just be the icing on the rotten Christmas cookie."

John came to his feet and walked over to her. Placing his hands on her shoulders, he turned her to look at him. "It wasn't you, sweetheart. It was me. When your mom left, grandma wanted us to move in with her—but there were conditions and rules and I just knew it wasn't the kind of environment I wanted you to grow up in."

"Dad, I know all this. I remember the fights but…what made her hate Christmas?"

He shook his head. "She didn't. As far as I know, she always loved it."

"Then…then why? Why would she ruin ours?"

A sad expression covered his face. "It was punishment. I grew up loving Christmas and we always made such a big celebration out of it. It was her way of punishing me for not falling in line. She took away that joy."

Tears filled Melanie's eyes. "See? She was hateful. And whatever this cabin thing is, I don't want it."

"Mel…"

"No, I'm serious!" she interrupted. "I don't want anything from her. She ruined so many things in our lives because she was being spiteful! Why on earth would I accept anything from her?"

"Because I think you need it," he said, his tone firm, serious.

"Excuse me?"

Leading her back to the sofa, they sat down. "I think this may have come at the perfect time."

She rolled her eyes. "Seriously?"

"Okay, that didn't quite come out the way I had planned," he said with a chuckle. "What I meant is…I think you could really use the time away. With the pressure you're feeling about the book, maybe a change of scenery will really help put things into perspective."

"Dad," Melanie began, "a change of scenery is not going to undo twenty-five years of hating

Christmas. And besides, I really don't want the…the cabin. I don't want anything from her. It would have meant more to me to have her in my life while she was alive."

He sighed. "I know and I wish things could have been different. But…this is really something you need to do."

She looked at him with disbelief. "Now I *need* to do it? Why?"

"Melanie, you are my daughter and I love you."

"That's an ominous start."

"You're too young to be this disillusioned and angry. We can't go back and change anything, but I think you need to do this to make peace with the past and have some hope for the future."

"Dad…"

"Three months, Mel, that's all I'm asking."

She jumped to her feet. "You expect me to go live in some arctic place for three months? Are you crazy?"

He smiled patiently at her. "I'm not crazy and you know I'm right."

"No…I'm still going with crazy."

"There's a stipulation in the will," he began cautiously.

"What kind of stipulation?"

"You need to live in the cabin for three months. After that, you're free to sell it."

"That's a bunch of bull. What if I don't want to live there at all? Why can't I just sell it now? Or give it away?"

"If you don't want it, it will be given away."

"Well then…good riddance."

"You're being spiteful just for the sake of it, Mel. What have you got to lose? You work from home so you don't have that hanging over your head and your condo is paid for. Think of it as a writing retreat. Your editor will love the idea and it will show how you're seriously trying to get the book done. It's a win-win if you think about it."

"Ugh," she sighed. "I'm not a big fan of being cold."

"The cabin has heat."

"It will mean I'll be gone for Christmas."

He chuckled. "Nice try. We don't celebrate it anymore, remember?"

She let out a small growl of frustration. "I'm still going to have writer's block. That's not going to change."

"Trust me. It will."

Tilting her head, she gave him a curious look. "What's that supposed to mean?"

"Okay, there really isn't any way *not* to tell you this…"

"Tell me what?"

"The town is pretty much all about Christmas."

"Forget it. I'm not going." She sat back down and crossed her arms.

"You're too old to pout so knock it off," he said.

She glared at her father. "So I'm supposed to go to this…this…Christmas town and then, thanks to the wonder of it all, suddenly I'm going to be able to write this fabulous holiday story and have it become a bestseller?"

"There's that imagination again! I knew it was still in there!"

"Ha-ha. Very funny." Slouching down she let out another growl. "I really don't want to do this."

"Mel, it's not often that I put my foot down. You're normally more level-headed and you're old enough that I don't need to, but this time, I'm going to have to put my foot down."

"Who gets the cabin if I turn it down?"

John sighed dejectedly. "I have no idea. The lawyer didn't say."

"Maybe she left it to someone who really needs it," Melanie said, trying to sound hopeful.

"She did," John replied. "You."

****

A week later, Melanie was in her car and driving halfway across the country to see if she could get her writing mojo back. It was a fifteen-hour drive so she split it up over two days and since she was alone in the car, she had nothing to do but think.

"She couldn't have left me a condo in Hawaii or maybe someplace tropical like the Bahamas? No. I have to go to the tip of freaking New York for this." It was a running dialogue in her head throughout the drive and it seemed like the closer she got, the angrier she became.

On the second day of the trip, when her GPS told her she was less than an hour away from her destination, she called her father and put him on speakerphone.

"Hey, sweetheart! How's the drive?"

"She hated me," Melanie replied. "She seriously hated me."

"I'm not even going to pretend I don't know who you're referring to," he said. "Are you there already? Is the cabin in bad shape?"

"I'm not there yet but I'm driving on this little two-lane road and there is nothing out here. I mean nothing! The GPS says I should be there soon but I haven't seen a city or a town in quite a while. Where am I supposed to shop and get food? Or am I supposed to hunt for it? Because if I am, that's a deal-breaker and you should have told me."

John laughed. "You seriously need to put all of this in your book. It's hysterical!"

"I'm not trying to be funny here, Dad! I'm serious! There isn't anything around!"

"You haven't gotten there yet. If I remember correctly, there are plenty of places to shop and eat. You won't starve and you certainly won't have to go out and kill your dinner so don't worry."

"But you don't know that for sure…"

"Mel, stop looking for trouble. We talked about this. It's going to be good for you. Your editor is thrilled and promised to give you a little extra time so you're off to a promising start."

"Yeah…I'm lucky," Melanie deadpanned.

"You need a positive attitude, young lady," he admonished. "I'm serious. I want you to make the most of this time you have up there."

She mentally sighed. "I'll try, Dad. But I'm not making any promises."

"That's all I ask."

"Okay, well…let me go because the road seems to be getting pretty winding and hilly and I need to pay attention to it. I'll call you when I get there."

"Be safe, sweetheart!"

Hanging up, Melanie frowned at the road. It was getting narrower and the sky was getting a little bit darker. A chill went down her spine and attributing it to the cooling temperatures, she cranked up the heat.

The GPS began calling out directions to her and Melanie feared she was leaving civilization further and further behind. "I better hit the *New York Times* for this," she murmured. A few minutes later she hit the brakes and stared at the giant sign on the side of the road.

"Silver Bell Falls Welcomes You!"

Melanie frowned and then looked around because she was certain she was hearing things. Turning down her car stereo, she groaned when she heard the song "Silver Bells" coming from the massive sign.

City sidewalks, busy sidewalks, dressed in holiday style…in the air there's a feeling of Christmas…

"You have got to be kidding me." Cranking the radio up to block out the Christmas carol, Melanie slammed her foot on the gas and continued her drive. It was maybe only a mile down the road when she spotted a small grocery store, a gas station and a diner.

And that was it.

"I guess I just drove through town," she sighed. It was tempting to stop and look around but she was anxious to get to the house and check it out first. Being practical, Melanie had already shopped for enough food and essentials to get her by for the first night. And besides, she had no idea what kind of shape the house was going to be in.

"Turn left," the GPS directed and Melanie did just that. "Your destination is at the end of the road."

Squinting, Melanie looked straight ahead but saw…nothing. There were trees, lots and lots of trees. Slowing down, she approached the end of the pavement and saw a dirt road that led through the trees and a small mailbox hidden in the brush.

"Charming." With no other choice, she carefully drove off the pavement and made her way over the bumpy road through the trees. It was like a dense forest and for a minute, she didn't think she was going to get through it.

But then she did.

The field opened up and off to the right was a house—not a cabin. In her mind, Melanie pictured some sort of log cabin, but the structure she was looking at was more stone than log. It was a one-story home with a wraparound porch and a red roof. The yard was completely manicured and the place even looked like it had a fresh coat of paint.

Since neither she nor her father had any contact with her grandmother, there was no way for them to know about the upkeep on the place. She had tried to question the lawyer, but other than giving her the deed to the house and the keys, he had very little information for her.

A little beyond the house was a shed. It looked like it was perched on a trailer and it certainly looked a lot newer than the house. Maybe it had been a new addition. Maybe her grandmother hadn't known she was going to die and was doing some renovations on the property.

Pulling up to the front of the house, Melanie sighed. She was anxious to go and explore the space and silently prayed she wasn't going to open the door to some sort of nightmare. Climbing from the car, the first thing she did was stretch. Looking around the property from where she stood, the only thing that was obvious to her was that she had no neighbors—she couldn't even see another house!

Pulling the key from her pocket, she closed the car door and carefully walked up the two steps to the front porch. Stopping at the front door, she bounced on her feet and noticed that the floor was in pretty good shape—no creaking and a lot of the wood looked fairly new.

Not a bad start, she thought and opened the front door.

Stopping dead in her tracks, she could only stare. It was dark and dusty and there was a smell that made her want to gag. Not that she was surprised, but it did cause her to spring into action. With a hand over her mouth, she quickly made her way around the house opening windows. Next, she went out to her car and grabbed the box of cleaning supplies out of the trunk. Melanie knew a certain amount of cleaning would be involved, but she hadn't expected quite so much.

For the next three hours she scrubbed and dusted and vacuumed and mopped. It didn't matter that it was thirty degrees outside, and currently pushing that temperature inside thanks to the open windows; she was sweating. Once she was satisfied with the way things looked, she walked outside, grabbed the box of linens and went about making the bed. Next came the groceries and finally her own personal belongings.

It was dark outside and every inch of Melanie's body hurt. Slowly she made her way back around the house to close the windows and jacked up the heat. Luckily the fireplace was gas, clearly a recent update. She flipped the switch and sighed with relief when it roared to life and the blower immediately began pushing out heat as well.

Guzzling down a bottle of water, she looked around with a sense of satisfaction. The house was small, maybe only a thousand square feet, but it had potential. Grabbing a banana from her cooler, she peeled and ate it while contemplating her next move.

"Shower," she finally said. "A nice hot shower or maybe a bath." The latter sounded far more appealing. Locking the front door, Melanie walked to the newly-cleaned bathroom and started the bath water. It was a fairly decent-sized tub and for that she was grateful. "Bath salts," she murmured and padded to the master bedroom to search through her toiletry bag.

Within minutes, the bathroom was steamy and fragrant and Melanie could feel the tension starting to leave her body. Her cell phone rang and she cursed when she realized she had forgotten to call her father when she'd arrived.

"Hey, Dad!" she said quickly. "Sorry!"

He chuckled. "Are you all right?"

"I am. The house was a mess and once I got inside and looked around, I couldn't help but start cleaning. I guess I lost track of the time."

"Have you eaten dinner yet?" he asked expectantly.

"A banana."

"Mel…" he whined. "You have to start taking better care of yourself."

"I will. I know. Actually, I'm just getting ready to take a nice hot bath to relax. I promise I'll eat as soon as I'm done."

He sighed wearily. "Okay. Be sure that you do. Call me tomorrow."

"I will, Dad. Thanks."

She hung up and turned the water off. Looking around, Melanie grabbed some fresh towels from one of her boxes and set them on the vanity before stripping down and gingerly climbing into the steamy water. A groan of pure appreciation escaped her lips as soon as she was fully submerged.

"This almost makes up for all the grime," she sighed and rested her head back, closing her eyes. "Heavenly."

For a few minutes, Melanie let her mind be blank and simply relaxed. The hot water and the salts were doing wonders for her tired body and it was glorious. Then, unable to help herself, her mind went back into work mode. A running list of supplies she was going to need was first and she cursed not having a pad and pen handy to start writing things down. Next came the necessities of going into town and maybe meeting her neighbors.

And then there was the book.

The groan that came out this time had nothing to do with relaxation and everything to do with dread. "Damn Christmas story. Why can't I write what I want to write?" It was something she'd been asking her editor for months and the only response she got was how all of the other in-house authors were contributing to building their holiday line, and she would be no exception. "Stupid rule."

And then something came to her.

Melanie sat up straight in the tub and only mildly minded the water that sloshed over the side of the tub. "All I need to do is write a story that takes place around Christmas. It doesn't have to necessarily be about Christmas!" Her heart began to beat frantically. "I've been focusing on the wrong thing!" Relief swamped her and she forced herself to relax again. Sinking back into the water, she closed her eyes and let her mind wander to all of the possibilities that had suddenly opened up.

"A romance at Christmas time," she said quietly. "Major emphasis on romance, minor on Christmas.

Technically, I'm meeting my obligations." She smiled. "Hmm…a heroine alone—maybe stranded—in a winter storm and a sexy hero who storms in and rescues her."

Melanie purred. "Yeah. That could definitely work." Sinking further down into the water, an image of the hero came to mind. Tall. That was a given. Muscular, but not overly so. Maybe lean would be a better way to describe him. And dark hair. She was a sucker for the dark hair. "Sex on a stick," she said quietly, enjoying the image that was playing in her mind.

The bathroom door swung open and Melanie's eyes flew open as she screamed. The man standing in the doorway seemed to have stepped almost completely from her imagination. If she wasn't so freaking scared at the moment, she would appreciate it.

"I wouldn't count on sex on a stick or anyplace else if I were you. You're trespassing and you're under arrest."

Chapter Two

For a moment, Josiah could only stare.

There was a naked woman in Carol Harper's tub.

Holy. Crap.

When he'd driven up to his place a few minutes ago and saw the strange car parked out in front of the cabin, he immediately became suspicious. Hazards of the job, considering he was the sheriff of Silver Bell Falls. The front door had been locked and the blinds drawn just as they always were, but the car was definitely a red flag. So he let himself in.

And found the naked woman he was currently staring at.

"Who the hell are you?" she demanded, strategically covering herself so he couldn't see what he already saw.

Like he was going to forget *that* any time soon.

"You need to step out of the tub, Miss…?"

"Oh, right," she snapped. "You break into my house and I'm supposed to listen to what you have to say? I'll call the cops! You have no right breaking in here and…"

"Wait, wait, wait," he interrupted. "Your house? I don't think so."

She rolled her eyes. "Look, can you…can you just turn around or something so I can get out of this tub and put some clothes on?"

His immediate thought was to say no, but there was no way she was going to get by him—certainly not while she was naked and wet. Wordlessly, he turned his back to her and almost instantly heard the water begin to drain and then the gentle splashing as she rose.

"Um…without turning around, could you hand me a towel? I can't reach it."

It was almost as if the universe was mocking him. He hadn't been with a woman in over a year and now he had one soaking wet and naked two feet away and he had to arrest her. Yeah, sometimes life really sucked.

Behind him, she cleared her throat and Josiah turned around. He swallowed hard at the sight of her. Her dark brown hair was twisted up into some sort of messy knot and she had the lightest blue eyes he had ever seen.

And right now they were shooting daggers at him.

"You're going to need to put something on other than a towel," he said. "I'm not bringing you down to the station in just a towel."

Crossing her arms, she cocked a hip and smirked. "I hate to break it to you Ace, but you're not bringing me anywhere. This is *my* house and *you* are the one who is trespassing. Now I'll ask you nicely to leave, but if you refuse, I *will* call the cops and I *will* have you arrested."

He couldn't help the bark of laughter that came out. "Sweetheart, I can't arrest myself. And I know the owner of this house personally and believe me, that isn't you."

"Then you knew my grandmother. She willed the house to me," Melanie said smugly, arching a dark brow at him defiantly.

"She…willed?" Josiah asked. "That would mean…I…"

"She passed away almost a month ago," she supplied softly. "This cabin was willed to me. I just got in late this afternoon."

"No one told me…," he stammered, his whole posture going lax. Leaning against the vanity, he looked at her. "I'm sorry for your loss. Carol was a real nice woman."

He didn't expect her own roar of laughter.

"I'm sorry…did I miss something?" he asked.

"My grandmother was many things. Nice wasn't one of them." Without another word, she stepped around him and walked out of the bathroom.

Josiah stared after her until he heard a door slam. Swiping a hand over his weary face, he muttered a curse and stepped out of the room and went to wait out in the living room. Hopefully she was going to come back out and talk to him.

Ten minutes later, she did.

"You're still here?" she asked, walking into the kitchen and pulling open the refrigerator.

He walked over and stood on the opposite side of the breakfast bar. "Were you expecting me to leave?"

"Hoping is the word I'd use." Her words were firm, but there was a slight tilt to her lips as she said it.

"Sorry to disappoint but being that we're neighbors, I figured I'd better introduce myself."

She looked at him quizzically. "Neighbors? I didn't see another house around here."

"Right next door," he said, walking over to the front window. "You can see my house from here."

Walking over, she looked out the window and frowned. "You live in the shed?"

He chuckled. "It's not a shed, it's a…it's a tiny house." He hated the phrase but it was all the rage right now and unless he said it, most people didn't know what he was talking about.

She looked at him and didn't bother to hide the smirk. "A tiny house? Seriously?"

"I didn't name it," he said with a hint of irritation. "That's what they're called."

"Okay. Whatever," she said and walked back to the kitchen.

"Look, we obviously got off on the wrong foot. No one told me about your grandmother and I was only doing my job."

"Your job?"

"I'm the sheriff of Silver Bell Falls. Josiah Stone." He held out a hand to her and couldn't help but smile when she looked at it with a hint of disdain.

"Melanie Harper," she finally said and shook his hand. "The sheriff, huh?"

He nodded. "At your service."

She chuckled and turned back to the refrigerator. "I'm not trying to be rude, but all I've had to eat today is a bowl of cereal for breakfast and a banana for dinner. I'm sorry I freaked you out by being here, but as you can tell by the looks of the place, I'm settling in."

He pulled up a stool at the breakfast bar and studied her. "The look of the place doesn't tell me anything. I didn't know Carol had planned on leaving the place to you."

"Oh? You talked about it with her?"

He nodded again. "As a matter of fact, I did."

Melanie straightened and looked at him. "Really? Why?"

"Because I wanted to buy the property from her. I've been trying to buy the property from her for years but she always refused to sell and she never told me why." He shook his head with a grin. "Now I know."

"Is that why you have your…what is it…teeny house out there on the property?"

"It's a *tiny* house," he corrected, "and even though she wouldn't sell, she did allow me to use the land. I just always thought she'd eventually cave and sell it to me."

"Yeah, well…that was my grandmother, the puppet master."

"I don't think I'd say that…"

"Trust me. I would," Melanie said, and leaned against the countertop and looked at him. "I'll tell you what, I have to honor her nutty last wishes and stay here for three months. After that, I'm out of here. I'll sell it to you then."

He eyed her suspiciously. "Just like that? You don't even know me."

She shrugged. "Don't care. I don't want to be here but I have to. If you want the place so bad, consider it yours."

"And all I have to do is wait three months?"

"I won't even argue the price with you. All I ask is that you be fair."

"How do I know you won't change your mind?" he asked, still feeling suspicious.

Stepping away from the counter, Melanie walked closer to him. "For starters, I didn't want to come here. I live in North Carolina and I love it there. Next, I don't like the cold. This whole living near Canada thing? I already hate it. Then there's the whole Christmas thing."

"What Christmas thing?"

"There is no way I want to live in a town called Silver Bell anything. I hear you guys make it feel like Christmas all year long."

Josiah smiled. "That we do. It's wonderful. We have festivals and fairs and…"

"Save it," she interrupted. "I don't do Christmas so there's no way I'd stay here. Festivals and fairs are of no interest to me."

He looked at her like she was crazy. "What do you mean you don't *do* Christmas? What the hell does that even mean?"

"Look…Josiah?" she asked and he nodded. "It's late, I'm starving and it's been a really long day. I really don't have it in me to go into all of this right now. So if you wouldn't mind…"

"I've got a pizza," he said.

"Wait…what?"

"Pizza. Out in the car."

She shook her head and laughed. "It's probably frozen by now."

"That's what an oven's for. Come on. I'll share it with you and we can be neighborly and get to know one another."

Melanie looked at him and frowned. "I appreciate the offer but…"

Josiah moved quickly and was standing right in front of her in the blink of an eye. "You have to say yes. You owe me."

Her eyes went wide. "Excuse me?" she asked incredulously. "How is it exactly that I owe you anything?"

"Well if it wasn't for you, I would be enjoying a hot pizza right now," he said casually. "Now, thanks to you, I had to get back into sheriff mode and nearly ruined my dinner. So, like I said, you owe me."

He knew the instant he had her because her lips began to twitch with a smile.

"You're crazy," she said, shaking her head as her smile grew.

"Yeah, but we're neighbors now and soon you'll be selling me the property. Wouldn't you like to know it's going to someone decent?"

"You really don't want an answer to that one," she replied and took a step back. "I…um…I haven't finished unpacking or anything and I don't know if there are dishes here or if they're even usable."

"Not to worry. Why don't I bring the pizza in and you can heat it up and I'll go next door and grab plates and napkins and all that good stuff? What do you say?"

She was still chuckling. "I still say you're crazy but I'm starving so how can I say no?"

He smiled at her, deciding instantly that he liked her and couldn't wait to get to know a little more about her. "I'll be right back."

He stepped out the front door, closing it behind him, and let out a deep breath. Carol Harper was dead and a wave of sadness hit him. No matter what her granddaughter thought, Carol was a good woman, a generous woman.

He just wished he knew why she reneged on the deal she promised to make him for the property. She turned him down time and time again whenever he brought up the subject, but she promised she'd let him be the first to put an offer in when the time came. Unfortunately, she never mentioned she was leaving it to her granddaughter.

Hell, she never even mentioned that she had a granddaughter!

With a shake of his head, he walked over to his car and grabbed the pizza. He chuckled when he looked at the box and had a feeling Melanie Harper was going to give him a little hell for it.

He couldn't wait.

****

Melanie looked at the box in Josiah's hands and then back at him. "It's a frozen pizza."

He nodded.

"But I…you…" She sighed with frustration. "You led me to believe you had an actual pizza out there in the car!"

"Technically, you just assumed I had a hot pizza in the car," he corrected.

"No, you said I ruined your dinner. That implied you had purchased the pizza hot and now it was cold."

He shrugged. "I just meant that because of you I missed eating dinner while watching one of my favorite shows." He placed the pizza down on the counter and turned to leave. "That one cooks at 400 degrees for about twenty minutes. I'm gonna go home and grab a quick shower and the plates and all and I'll be back before it's ready."

"So now I'm making you dinner?" she demanded, annoyance coursing through her. When he didn't answer and continued to the door, she decided she'd had enough. "You know what, I think I'll pass on the neighborly thing. You can take your pizza and make it at home. I'll find something here."

Josiah stopped at the door and sighed before turning around to face her. "Are you always this difficult or is it just me?"

Crossing her arms over her chest, Melanie looked at him defiantly. "Just you."

He walked back across the room toward her. "Why? I'm just trying to be a nice guy and offer to share my dinner with you. I'm not seeing a problem here."

"You broke into my house, disturbed my bath and threatened to arrest me! You don't see a problem with any of that?"

He chuckled and shrugged again. "I thought we'd moved on from that."

"It just happened!" she cried.

"Like fifteen minutes ago. Sheesh. Do you always hold grudges?" he asked innocently.

Melanie couldn't help it, she burst out laughing. This guy was clearly a little off his rocker but she was starving and nothing she had with her was going to be as good as the pizza—even though it was a frozen one. Dropping her arms and deciding to stop being defensive, she looked at him and smiled. "I can see there's no winning with you so I'll tell you what…go do what you have to do, I'll make the pizza and we'll start over when you get back. Deal?"

His smile grew as his deep brown eyes met hers and Melanie felt like every heroine she'd ever written about—her knees went a little weak and her tummy fluttered.

"Deal."

As soon as he was out the door, Melanie turned the oven on to get things going. In a way, she was grateful for Josiah's offer of dinner. All she had with her were some cans of soup, granola bars and fruit.

Pizza was infinitely better.

As she waited for the oven to preheat, she let herself go over the events of the last thirty minutes. She honestly thought she was going to have a heart attack when Josiah had burst into the bathroom on her. Here she was in a town she didn't know and all by herself—and let's not forget the whole naked-in-the-tub thing—and she was certain she was a goner. Shock was quickly overridden by anger when she realized who he was and what he thought! But looking back, she could now see why he did what he did and was kind of thankful that she now had someone looking out for her while she was here.

Plus, the bonus to it all is that she didn't have to look for a buyer for the place. All she had to do was get through the damn three months her grandmother had insisted on and then she would be rid of it. Hell, they could probably start drawing up the papers now! Making a mental note to call her grandmother's lawyer tomorrow, Melanie went and began to unwrap the pizza.

****

The hot water stung for a second before Josiah let himself relax in the small shower. As much as he liked his current home, he couldn't wait to build something more traditional in size and have a shower big enough for him to stretch out.

And possibly have someone to share it with.

Melanie's face instantly came to mind. Well, not just her face but the image of her in the bathtub. Yeah, that wasn't going to go away any time soon. She was beautiful and if he wasn't careful, he was going to find himself spending the night flirting with her rather than just trying to get to know her.

It was too soon to start thinking of her as anything but his new neighbor, but damn if he could forget everything he had already seen.

Quickly washing up, he wondered about her relationship with her grandmother. There was clearly a backstory there—and not a good one. He couldn't imagine the woman he had known for so many years doing anything that would make people dislike her, but apparently something had happened to cause a rift between the two of them. He could only hope Melanie would share the story with him.

Turning off the water, he stepped out, dried off and got dressed. In the kitchen, he scooped up some paper plates and napkins along with a couple of cans of soda. Normally he preferred beer with his pizza, but he didn't want to assume Melanie did too.

Checking the clock he saw twenty minutes had gone by so he made fast work of getting his boots on, grabbing his jacket and heading out the door. It took less than a minute to reach her front door. Rather than letting himself in, he knocked and waited for Melanie to answer.

"So you *are* familiar with the concept," she teased when she opened the door and Josiah knew exactly what she meant. Crazy how they seemed in sync like that already.

"I figured I'd try something new this time," he said with a lopsided grin. When she stepped aside, he walked in and could smell the pizza cooking. He held up the paper goods and drinks. "As promised."

"Thanks." She walked ahead of him back to the kitchen. "I have to admit, it wasn't until after you left that I worried about the oven. I mean, I have no idea the last time it was used or how the electric is in this place."

Josiah pulled up the stool he'd used earlier. "The place is in decent shape. Carol did a fairly good rehab job on the electric, heating and plumbing about five years ago."

Melanie looked around the place. "The whole place needs a good rehab."

He chuckled. "Yeah, most of the stuff in here is pretty outdated but the house itself is structurally sound. The rest is just cosmetic."

"I suppose. I really didn't want to invest any money in the place but if I'm going to be stuck here for three months, I want to be able to walk around without cringing."

"It's not that bad," he said lightly.

"Dark paneling on the walls, shag carpet…" Melanie shuttered. "It's not appealing at all."

"So do a little work on it and make it livable. It doesn't have to cost a whole lot," he suggested.

"Oh, sure. I do all the work and make this place nice and then you reap all the benefits of it," she said with a laugh. "No thanks. Maybe you should start working on it now since it's going to be yours in a few months."

"And let you reap all the benefits of my hard work while I'm living in the tiny house? No thanks."

They both laughed and when the timer on the oven buzzed, they worked together to get the pizza sliced and set up a place to eat.

"I hope you don't mind, but I thought maybe we could eat in the living room – you know, on the sofa," Melanie said. "It's more comfortable than this old kitchen set."

Josiah readily agreed. "Not to mention those chairs are really small. I was always afraid to sit in them."

They moved to the sofa and situated themselves and spent several moments in companionable silence while they ate. After the first slice, Melanie sighed. "Thank you," she said.

"For what?"

"This is so much better than soup. In my mind I had resigned myself to it, but my stomach was begging for something more."

He laughed. "I'm sure you'll go shopping tomorrow and start stocking up the place. There's a grocery store not far from here but if you wanted to go into the city, you're looking at about an hour's drive."

"Yikes," she said, reaching for her second slice. "I'm not used to being so isolated. Back home, everything is just minutes away from my house. I'm not sure I'll survive this."

Shrugging, Josiah reached for another slice. "You get used to it. It's kind of nice to have the peace and quiet surround you. No noise, no traffic...and in a town this size, everyone knows each other."

"That just seems weird."

"But true." He finished his slice and reached for another. "So what did your grandmother tell you about Silver Bell?"

Melanie finished chewing, grabbed a napkin and wiped her hands before answering. "She never told me anything. I haven't seen her since I was five."

Josiah froze and stared at her. "Excuse me?"

She nodded. "It's true. She and my dad had a falling out and they never saw each other again." She shrugged and took another slice. "Every couple of years, something would happen and they would try to talk but they'd end up arguing and then eventually they both just stopped."

"And she didn't try to have any contact with you?"

Melanie shook her head. "Nope. She cut us both out of her life. I hadn't really thought about her in years until my dad showed up a week ago to tell me she'd died and then about her will and this place."

"That is so weird," he murmured. "And very unlike the woman I knew."

"Just goes to show how you never really know with some people."

"I suppose…"

"Anyway, now I have to stay here for three months and then I can sell it according to the will. Kind of lucky that I ran into you, huh?"

"Oh, sure. Now you think it's luck. A little while ago, you were looking at it completely differently," he teased.

She laughed. "You barged in while I was naked in the tub! That one's gonna take a little while to get over!"

He leaned a little closer and waggled his eyebrows at her. "If you're hinting that you want to even the score and see me naked in the shower, all you have to do is ask!"

Playfully swatting him away, Melanie took a drink of her soda and quickly changed the subject. "So you're the sheriff of this place, huh?"

He nodded. "Sure am. I take care of the three thousand residents who call Silver Bell home." He took a drink and looked at her. "It's not a big city like you're obviously from, but it's a good place to live. I hope while you're here, you actually take some time to look around and meet some people."

Melanie made a non-committal sound. "How long have you been the sheriff?"

"Five years."

"Have you lived here your whole life?"

He nodded. "Born and raised. I moved away when I went to college but…the big city life held no appeal to me. Besides, I missed the food, the festivals and the closeness we have here."

"We are complete opposites," she said. "Raleigh is perfect for me because it's a big enough city where there is always something to do, everything is close by and no one has to know me if I don't want them to. I can blend into the crowd and do my own thing. It's great."

"So what is it that you do?"

"I'm a writer," she replied and looked over and saw he was waiting for more of an explanation—as most people did. "I write contemporary women's fiction."

"You mean romance?"

Melanie looked away and reached for her soda and nodded. "Yup. Go ahead and snicker and smirk and get it out of your system."

Frowning, he asked, "What's that supposed to mean?"

"It's what everyone does," she said mildly. "I say I write romance, people snicker and smirk and automatically assume I write porn or that I'm some sort of hack so…go ahead."

Putting his beverage down, Josiah turned on the sofa and faced her. "First of all, don't ever assume I'm like everyone else. I'm not. Secondly, I think it is incredibly cool that you write romance, or that you write anything! Hell, I could barely get through college because I couldn't write an essay! So the fact that you can sit down and write an entire book? I'm a little in awe of you right now."

She blushed and Josiah thought it was a good look on her. "Stop, you are not."

He nodded. "Yes, I am. I'm not a very creative or artistic person. I like dealing with the law because it is what it is —they're written down and rules are rules and I just follow them."

"What about hobbies? Do you like to read or paint or build or anything like that?"

He nodded again. "I do enjoy building things – but I follow a plan. I don't just sit down and come up with something." He shrugged. "My plan for the property was to buy it and build a house."

"Really?" she asked, surprise lacing her tone. "You're going to tear this place down?"

"No," he said. "I'm going to rehab it a bit and leave it as a guest house."

"Do you have a big family that you need a guest house?"

He chuckled. "I do, actually. I have two brothers and three sisters."

Her eyes went wide. "Wow! Seriously?"

"Sure do. What about you? Any siblings?"

She shook her head. "Only child."

When she didn't expand, Josiah decided it was a bit of a sore subject. "Anyway, so yes. I have a large family but I'm the only one who stayed here in Silver Bell. That's why a guest house would be a good thing."

"There's always the tiny house," she said and gave him a sassy smile. Josiah noticed she had dimples and when she relaxed, Melanie was capable of taking his breath away.

"Hey, don't knock the tiny house. It serves a good purpose and it's more up to date than this place."

"I'll take your word for it."

Looking down, he saw they had finished the pizza. He took a napkin and wiped his hands, then stood. "Come and see it."

She looked up at him. "What?"

"Come and see it," he repeated. "It's obviously not far and I think you'll be pleasantly surprised when you see how it is. You may actually want to change spaces with me," he said with a wink.

Laughing, Melanie stood. "I doubt it and besides, that would probably go against what my grandmother had in her will. I don't want to do anything to jeopardize that and miss out on selling you the place."

He shrugged. "I'd just have to make an offer to the next owner."

"Maybe," she said, tilting her head and studying him. "But they might not be as inclined to sell to you. They may want the place for themselves and tell you and your tiny house to find another place to live."

Josiah stepped in closer and had to resist the urge to touch her. "I'm beginning to think you have a thing against my tiny house," he teased. "I'm going to enjoy watching you gush over it."

"Gush?" she laughed but once her eyes met his, she almost instantly sobered. "I don't gush."

"We'll see," he said. And then because he simply couldn't help himself, he reached for her hand and pulled her toward the door. "Come on."

Neither bothered with a coat and Melanie let out a little shriek at the cold once they were outside.

"Oh stop," he said, gently pulling her along. "In ten feet you'll be inside." And sure enough, they reached the house and he went up the three steps, pulled the door open and motioned for her to go inside.

She paused in the doorway. "Oh." It was a breathy sigh.

He grinned because even though most people had that exact response when they first walked in, he somehow knew her response was genuine. He nudged her in a little more and closed the door. "Welcome to my home," he said, his voice low and a bit husky.

"I…I don't even know what to say," Melanie said quietly as she stepped into the room. "This is…wow." There was awe in her words and Josiah watched as she walked around the space and touched things and stopped to smile at pictures.

"Obviously…it's tiny," he said with just a hint of insecurity. He'd never brought anyone here—didn't want to hear the negative comments—but for some reason, he wanted Melanie to see it.

"I've seen these on TV," she said and turned and looked at him. "I watch a lot of HGTV."

He looked at her oddly. "What's HGTV?"

She shook her head and chuckled. "Do you get cable or satellite TV out here?"

He nodded. "We're not so out of touch here in Silver Bell, you know." He meant to sound offended but he couldn't help his own laugh.

"It's the house and garden network. They do a lot of DIY shows and home makeover things. The tiny house movement is huge right now and they have several shows dedicated to it. I've just never seen one in person. It's really rather impressive." Melanie sat on the sofa and then got up and moved to the kitchen.

"It's not for everyone," he said quickly, noticing the way she was moving around as if trying to figure out how to maneuver in the space.

"Neither are big houses," she said. "I'm not saying I could function in this kitchen in the long-term, but I think everything here works just fine." She smiled at him. "I mean, you're not going to host a big dinner party with a kitchen this small, but it's perfect for two."

He was about to comment that it was only him and then wondered if she'd realized what she said. She moved over to look in the bathroom and merely popped her head in and then out again. Looking at him over her shoulder, she said, "That would be the deal-breaker."

"The bathroom really is small," he said.

"Oh, I don't mind a small bathroom, but I would die without a big shower—or a tub! I have both back home so I know I'm a little spoiled but that shower certainly looked…"

"Tiny?" he supplied.

Melanie laughed. "I really wish there were another word to use!"

"Tell me about it," he said, laughing with her. "It's not the manliest word to keep tossing around."

"You must get ribbed about it quite a bit."

He shook his head. "I really don't talk about this place with many people. My family knows what it's called but to anyone else I just say I live in a small bungalow."

"Hmm…I don't know. That doesn't have a manly sound to it either," she teased. She looked around. "Where do you sleep?"

Josiah pointed to the ladder. "There's a sleeping loft up there."

"Oh."

"You can climb up and look," he said. "It's not much and you can't stand up once you get up there."

"So you basically climb the ladder and then crawl into the bed?"

He nodded.

"That's not always a bad thing," she said as she carefully climbed the ladder. "Although, I think I would have opted for stairs."

"They took up more space," he said. "Although they would have provided storage and drawers, I wanted floor space more."

Melanie was perched near the top and looking at the loft. "It's really kind of cool. And you have a skylight! On a starry night, that's not a bad view to have."

Looking up at her and the way her skinny jeans were hugging her bottom, Josiah was pretty damn thrilled with his current view.

He stepped back as she climbed down but not far enough. Once she turned, they were nearly toe-to-toe. Josiah couldn't help but inhale deeply. The woman was walking temptation and she smelled incredible. The urge to lean forward, to close the distance between them was so strong and by the way Melanie was looking at him, he knew she felt it too.

"Josiah?" she asked, her voice a near whisper.

He cursed his damn morals and stepped back. She really didn't know him and he didn't know her and no matter how attracted he was to her—and he was—there was no way he would act on it this soon. When he kissed her, he was going to know her for more than an hour.

Melanie must have sensed his reluctance because her expression mirrored his own—still. Clearing his throat, he tried to sound casual. "Let me walk you home and help you clean up."

"It's only ten feet away. I think I'll be all right." Her tone was soft and light but he could still see a trace of disappointment there.

Or was it wishful thinking?

"I insist. I made you cook and we sort of walked out before cleaning up." Without waiting, he walked to the front door and stepped out, holding it open for her. Melanie followed and silently they walked back to her house and began to clear away the dinner mess. When it was all cleared up, he turned to her. "Do you have any plans for tomorrow?"

She shook her head. "Not really. I need to go into town and do some food shopping but from what I saw, it won't be too hard to navigate." She laughed softly. "One grocery store doesn't give me many options."

"Well…if you'd like, I can go with you and show you around," he asked, hoping he wasn't sounding overly anxious.

"I saw the grocery store, the gas station and the diner," she said with a smirk. "Is there more to the town than that?"

He felt his own smile grow. "As a matter of fact there is. I'll tell you what, give me a couple of hours tomorrow and I'll show you all of the hidden treasures of Silver Bell."

Melanie's face was so expressive, he thought, that she couldn't hide her disbelief. "There are hidden treasures? Seriously?"

"Have I lied to you yet?"

She burst out laughing. "In the hour I've known you? No, I can't say that you have."

"Well then, there you go!" Josiah felt that pull again and forced himself to take another step back. "How about I meet you outside at eleven? That way you can sleep in if you want to."

Melanie smiled as her entire body seemed to relax. "Thank you. That would be nice."

"Okay," he said, nodding. Walking to the door, he turned around and looked at her one more time. "Sleep well, Melanie."

"Thanks for dinner," she said, walking toward him slowly.

Oh, no, he thought. If she got any closer, he wasn't so sure he wouldn't do something stupid, like kiss her.

"Sorry I scared you when I came in."

"Broke in," she corrected. "When you broke in."

He shrugged. "We'll have to agree to disagree." He took a steadying breath and opened the door. The cold air hit him full force and it worked as well as any cold shower ever had. "I'll see you in the morning. Good night."

Melanie had just reached the door and took it from his hands. "Good night."

Chapter Three

"And if you look over there on your right you'll see Silver Bell Park," Josiah said. "This is the main spot for any of the activities that involve the kids. Two years ago we had a generous donor who made it possible for us to put in all new playground equipment just in time for Christmas."

Melanie smiled and nodded and fought the urge to yawn. For over an hour Josiah had been driving her through town and every spot he brought to her attention was followed by a Christmas story. She was ready to lose her mind.

They turned the corner and Melanie noticed they were in a more populated part of town. There were small brick buildings and a few other shops and restaurants. She looked at Josiah questioningly. "How did I miss this coming into town?"

He chuckled. "It's not on the main route—although it should be."

She leaned forward and studied the buildings. "There are quite a few businesses here. I'm impressed."

"It's the town hall and chamber of commerce," he began, "and then the local utility companies. A few of the locals have businesses here as well." He paused and then slowed his truck down. "Right there is Bobby Cole's shop. He does appliance repair. Next to him is Stracey O'Neil's boutique. She sells all kinds of home goods like soaps and candles and that kind of stuff." Pointing across the street he said, "Over there is the salon. Dana, Shari and Jenny—they're sisters—own it. And next to it is Ava's Stationary. Oh, and on the corner is the ice cream parlor. They make it all on site and it's quite possibly the best ice cream in the world."

She looked at him and smiled. "Now I'm not so sure about that. I consider myself an ice cream aficionado and I'm going to have to try it for myself."

"Tell you what…why don't we grab some lunch at the diner and then we'll go over and have some ice cream for dessert. What do you say?"

Her immediate reaction was to say yes, but she hesitated. "Don't you have to work today?"

Josiah shook his head. "Nope. It's my day off."

"Well now I feel bad," she said.

"Why?"

"Because I'm sure you had other things to do on your day off and I've gone and monopolized your time. I'm sorry about that."

He pulled the truck over to the side of the road and put it in park before looking at her. "I realize we don't know each other very well but let me tell you a few things about me. One, I never do anything I don't want to do. Two, I'm extremely organized and therefore I rarely get behind on anything. Even if I take a day to do something unexpected, I'm not going to miss out on doing anything."

"You missed out on watching your favorite TV show last night while breaking into my house," she taunted sassily.

"When I was *checking* on a potential crime, I believe you meant to say," he replied. "And that was different. Besides, I recorded it."

"Okay. Fine. Whatever," she laughed.

"Three," he said, going back to his original conversation. "You aren't monopolizing my time. I offered to show you around town and that's exactly what I'm doing. We may not be a big city like you're used to, but I already knew how long it would take to show you everything and I had planned on us having lunch together. So it's not a big deal."

"Is there a four?"

"Does there need to be?" he teased. "I think I covered everything."

"Fair enough."

Seeming satisfied, Josiah put the truck in drive and drove the five minutes to the diner. It was an old mom-and-pop kind of place and Melanie thought it looked very retro and charming from the outside.

"If you'd like, before we head home later, we can go and do your food shopping. Then you don't have to come back into town."

She considered his offer for a minute and hesitated while chewing her bottom lip.

"I know what you're thinking," Josiah said, "and stop it. It's not a big deal and this is my normal day to grocery shop so we'd be killing two birds with one stone. All right?"

Melanie gave him a shy smile and followed him into the diner. "Get out of my head," she said softly as she walked by him. But secretly, she thought it was a little bit charming how he seemed to be able to read her so easily. It was a new feeling. A good one. None of the men she'd dated ever seemed to really get her and in less than twenty-four hours, Sheriff Josiah Stone knew her better than almost anyone.

Silver Bells…Silver Bells…it's Christmas time in the city…

She followed him across the restaurant and mentally groaned at the sound of Christmas carols playing over the sound system. Maybe if she tried really hard, she could tune them out. Unfortunately, when they sat, she found that there was a speaker almost directly over her head. And even if it weren't for the music, the entire place looked like the North Pole had thrown up in it. Every inch of wall space— and the ceiling—was covered in Christmas decorations. Melanie suddenly wished they had opted to skip lunch.

"Well hey there, Sheriff," the waitress said when she walked over to the booth they had chosen. "What a surprise to see you here on a Tuesday." She looked over at Melanie with blatant curiosity and then turned back to Josiah. "What can I get for you two today?"

"I'll start off with a coke, Bev," he said and then looked at Melanie.

"Oh, same for me," she said.

"Where are my manners," he began. "Bev, this is Melanie Harper. She's Carol's granddaughter and she's staying at the cabin for a while."

Bev's face lit up. "Is that right? Is Carol coming up to visit with you?"

A blush crept up Melanie's cheeks. "Um…she passed away. About a month ago."

Bev's hand fluttered over her heart and her expression instantly saddened. "Oh, sweetie, I'm so sorry. She was a good woman and she's going to be sorely missed around here."

Rather than comment the way she normally would have, Melanie accepted the condolences gracefully. "Thank you. It's nice to know she had so many friends here."

"Take your time looking at the menu and I'll be back in a minute with your drinks." With a subdued smile, she turned and walked away.

"That was very nice of you," Josiah said.

"What was?"

"Last night you pretty much held nothing back where your grandmother was concerned. You could have easily done the same thing here and you didn't."

Melanie shrugged. "What would be the point? It seems like the woman I knew and the woman you all knew were two different people. There's no point in me ruining everyone's memory of her."

Reaching across the table, Josiah took one of her hands in his and squeezed. "Like I said, it was very nice of you." He paused. "I hate that you and Carol had such a bad history. I wish you could have known her the way we all did. She helped a lot of people out around here—particularly at Christmas. There were some families who…"

"I don't want to talk about this," Melanie quickly interrupted. "I appreciate what you're trying to do, Josiah. I really do. But I don't really want to hear how wonderful she made other people's Christmases when she essentially ruined all of mine. She's one of the main reasons we don't even celebrate it anymore."

He pulled back and looked at her as if she were crazy. "What do you mean you don't celebrate it?"

"I think it's pretty self-explanatory. Christmas Eve and Christmas Day are just ordinary days to me and dad." She shrugged. "It's been that way for years."

"But…"

"Here you go," Bev said as she placed their drinks down on the table. "Have you had a chance to look at the menu?"

Melanie smiled at her apologetically. "Not yet but I'm going to right now. I'm starving!" And true to her word, she picked up the menu and began scanning it, ignoring Josiah's stare.

"Just give me a shout out when you're ready," Bev said and walked back toward the kitchen.

"What do you recommend?" Melanie asked him without looking up from the menu.

****

There were about a dozen questions whizzing around in Josiah's mind. Not celebrate Christmas? Because of Carol? How could that be? The woman was responsible for pretty much making sure every child in Silver Bell had at least one present under their Christmas tree. How could she have ignored her own granddaughter?

"I can hear you thinking from here," Melanie said without looking up from her menu. "It's not open for discussion, Josiah. We're having a nice day and I'd like to keep it like that. And if we are going to be neighbors for the next several months, I'd rather avoid fighting with you."

"I didn't plan on fighting," he said, but there was very little strength behind his words.

"Sure you were," she replied lightly, putting her menu down on the table. "It's kind of our thing." She smiled. "I'm going to have a BLT and fries. What about you?"

It was kind of their thing? Josiah wasn't sure how to respond to that, but she did have a point. They seemed to have to banter about everything. They didn't disagree in an angry way, but they certainly haven't agreed on much of anything. "Double cheeseburger and fries. My usual."

Melanie nodded. "I was tempted to order a salad just because we're going to get ice cream after this, but I haven't had a BLT in forever and…you know…bacon."

He chuckled. "It does make everything delicious."

Bev came back and took their orders and when they were alone again, Josiah wasn't sure what to say. He desperately wanted to know about her history with Carol, but knew that as of right now it was an off-limits topic. He hated small talk and yet…

"So what do you think of the town so far?" he asked.

"It's very different from Raleigh, I'll tell you that," she said with a laugh. "Not that it's a bad thing—I'm just not used to feeling so…isolated."

"It's not so bad. Most people who live here don't know any other way of life."

"You said your family doesn't live here anymore. Where did they move to?"

Settling back against the booth cushion, Josiah fought the urge to be childish and say it was off-limits. "Mom and dad retired down to Florida," he began.

"Mom said she had done her time with the long winters and the snow and wanted to experience life in the sunshine."

Melanie smiled. "Completely understandable."

He nodded. "Both of my brothers are down in Albany. "They're both tech guys and work for the same company now."

"Are they married?"

He nodded again. "Yup. And they both have kids." He shook his head. "They've always been a bit competitive with one another and it just seems like as soon as one does something, the other isn't too far behind. It's kind of entertaining to watch." He laughed. "Their wives thought it was funny at first, but I think it's losing some of its humor now that they seem to be mimicking each other's lives."

"I don't know," Melanie said, smiling at the image, "it takes some of the mystery out of what's in store for you and I think it could be pretty cool."

"Don't like surprises, huh?"

She shook her head. "I've had enough of them in my life, thank you very much. I wouldn't mind a crystal ball every now and then." Taking a sip of her soda, she gently pushed the glass aside. "And your sisters?"

"Excuse me?"

"Your sisters," she repeated. "You said you had three of them. Where are they at?"

Josiah took a sip of his own beverage before answering. "They're sort of scattered all over the place. Heather's down in Pennsylvania, married and just had her first baby. A girl—Dawn. Her husband is a high school teacher. Then there's Susan. She's down in Binghamton. Also married, no kids, and both she and her husband are in medical sales."

"Wow! That's kind of cool."

He shrugged. "They think so," he said with a smile. "And the baby of the family is my sister Danielle. She's the feisty one. It's funny because she's this tiny little thing but she can kick all of our butts." He laughed. "Her husband is a professional football player—he's about a foot or so taller than her—and I think he's intimidated by her too!"

"Now there's an image!" Melanie said, laughing with him. "What does she do?"

"Actually, the two of you have a little something in common; she's a writer too."

"Really? What does she write?"

"She does the life and style articles for their local newspaper. She really doesn't need to work but she loves writing."

"When it's in your blood, you know it and you find any creative outlet you can find to get it out there."

He studied her for a moment. "How'd you get started?"

Melanie imitated his pose and relaxed back against the seat. "It was a case of pure luck."

"What do you mean?"

"I entered a writing contest while I was in college," she said. "It was to pitch a book idea to a publisher." She shrugged. "They loved it. I got signed to write the book and it sold relatively well so they offered me a three-book deal and I readily took it."

"Wow! That's impressive!"

She gave him a small smile. "Yeah…it sounds like it but for those first few years I still needed to have a day job. So I worked in retail and did some waitressing for a while—and found out I'm not very good at it—and after the fourth book, I was able to do it full-time."

"And again I say…impressive," Josiah said. "So what are you working on now? Anything?"

"Actually, it's part of the reason why I'm here. I'm treating my time here as a writing retreat." Pausing, she sighed. "For the first time in my life, I have writer's block. My publisher and editor and agent are all at the end of their ropes with me."

Leaning forward, Josiah rested his elbows on the table and looked at her with concern. "What do you think is causing it?"

She waved him off. "It's not really important. Anyway, I think I had a bit of a breakthrough last night. It sort of came to me while I was in the tub."

She looked up and gave him a pointed look. "Before someone broke in and disturbed me."

"You're never going to let that go, are you?"

Melanie playfully shook her head. "It's not everyday someone barges in on me while I'm taking a bath."

It was on the tip of his tongue to say something about how amazing it was for him, but decided to keep it to himself. "You have to admit, you'll never forget our first meeting," he teased with a wink.

She burst out laughing and Josiah found he loved the sound of it. He joined her and before either could say anything else, Bev was back with their lunches.

They ate in companionable silence and Josiah knew right then and there, he'd more than likely never forget Melanie Harper.

****

"I think I've died and gone to heaven."

"I told you."

"No," she said, "you made it all sound rather blasé…but this?" She held her chocolate ice cream cone out toward him. "This is decadent perfection."

"I said it was the best ice cream in the world. How is that blasé?"

"There was no passion in your voice. Ice cream like this deserves a little passion." It wasn't until the words were out that Melanie actually heard them and she wanted to groan and perhaps die of embarrassment. Was she seriously sitting in Josiah's truck talking about passion with him? What in the world?

"I keep telling Nikki—she's the owner—she better make sure her daughters know the family recipe because she can never close the shop."

"How many does she have?"

"Four—Kathy, Donna, Caroline and Rhonda. So chances are good that they'll be in business for a good long time. Her ice cream alone makes living here worthwhile."

"That and the fact it wasn't like Christmastown in there."

He chuckled. "Geez, woman. Ease up on the Christmas hate. While you're here, you better learn to embrace it. It's going to be everywhere."

"Hate to break it to you, but Silver Bell hasn't cornered the market on that. Everywhere you go from November first to December thirty-first is all trussed up for Christmas."

"So what does that mean? You don't leave the house for two months?"

She glared at him, but found it hard to be truly angry. "No," she said and then took a few licks of her cone. "I just limit my outings and keep my iPod handy at all times."

"Anyone ever tell you you're a Scrooge?"

With a smile and wink, Melanie nodded. "For two months out of every year!"

Josiah laughed out loud. "You sound very proud of that fact!"

"You have no idea."

They pulled up in front of the cabin and Josiah parked but didn't move to get out. Turning in his seat, he faced Melanie. "I had a really good time today."

She faced him with a smile of her own. "I did too."

"You sound surprised."

She shrugged. "I don't know…I think I had such a negative attitude about being here that I didn't think I'd find anything good about it." She paused. "Then you added to it last night…"

He rolled his eyes and groaned. "Okay, let's make a deal right now—neither of us is allowed to bring it up anymore. We've talked it to death and it was all an unfortunate misunderstanding and I think it's safe to say we can move on."

Melanie considered him for a minute. "I don't know…"

"What? What's wrong with that?"

She shrugged. "You sort of made out better than I did in the whole thing."

"How do you figure?"

"You walked in and saw me naked! I was mortified! You came out of the whole thing unscathed!"

"So if you walked in on me naked, would we be even?"

Her mind instantly raced with possibilities. Normally, Melanie was the type of woman who didn't make rash decisions and weighed all of her options. But something about Josiah Stone made her want to throw all of that away and act rashly and recklessly and not worry about the consequences. See him naked? She did last night in her dreams.

Beside her, Josiah cleared his throat. Melanie looked at him and saw the smirk on his face and felt herself blush.

"The fact that you didn't immediately shut me down tells me you're considering it," he said silkily.

Melanie's eyes met his and she saw heat there and knew it mirrored her own. She was stuck here for three months and then she'd be gone. Could she possibly let go and let herself enjoy her time here and have it include the sexy sheriff?

"At the end of three months I'm going back to North Carolina," she blurted out.

Josiah seemed to know exactly what she was implying. "So you've said."

"It's true. I…I don't normally get involved with someone when I know it's going to be short-term."

He nodded. "I was offering you the chance to see me naked. I wasn't trying to talk you into changing your life or making a commitment."

"Oh," she said quietly. "I mean…okay…that's good." She nodded quickly and fidgeted with the door handle. "Um…we should probably get those groceries inside." When she went to open the door, Josiah's hand on her arm stopped her. For a brief moment, Melanie was afraid to meet his gaze.

"Hey," he said softly and waited until she did finally look up at him. "I think I'm as out of my comfort zone right now as you are. I don't…what I mean is…I don't usually tease like this. In the past, I had a tendency to take things slowly and see where it led. But I look at you, Melanie, and I don't want to wait and see. The clock is already ticking and if that means throwing caution to the wind and jumping in with both feet right now so we spend as much time as we can together until you leave, then I'm willing to do that."

Her eyes went a little wide at his words. "I wasn't expecting you," she said, gazing at his face in wonder.

Josiah leaned in closer. "I wasn't expecting you either, but now that you're here, I'm extremely grateful."

A small sigh of relief at his words had Melanie relaxing a bit. "This is crazy," she whispered. "We don't even know each other."

"And yet we seem to know each other quite well. When we talk, it's like I know what you're going to say. You can read my mind and it's the same for me. We can sit here and question it and try to make sense of it, but all we're doing is cheating ourselves out of time where we could be together."

"We're together right now…"

He shook his head. "You know what I'm saying." With a sigh, he pulled back. "Just…promise me you'll think about it."

As if she'd be able to think of anything but.

Without another word, they each climbed from the truck. Josiah helped her carry her groceries into the cabin before taking care of his own. Melanie wanted to ask if he was going to come back over when he was done, but she knew she needed some time to think about what they had just discussed. As much as she wanted to be that carefree person, she knew she'd need a little time to think.

With the last bag in her hand, Josiah turned and faced her, stepping in close. "I'm not going to rush you or push," he said softly. "You know where I stand on this. And if you think it's something you'd like to…explore, I'll be right over here waiting." And before she knew it, he leaned in and placed a gentle kiss on her cheek before turning and walking away.

Waiting until Josiah was in his tiny house, Melanie let out the breath she was holding. Holy heck…what was she supposed to do now? Turning, she walked into the cabin and closed the door behind her. She moved around putting food away as if in a trance.

Three months.

She had three months away from her normal life to be…whatever she wanted to be. Sure there was her writing and her deadline that needed to be dealt with, but it wasn't as if she and Josiah would be spending every waking moment together. She really did enjoy his company and other than his seemingly ridiculous love of living in this tiny Christmas-themed town, she also really liked him.

He was sexy and attractive and Melanie knew— she just knew—she would never regret the time she spent with him.

In and out of bed.

Whoa…getting a little ahead of yourself, aren't you? "Actually, I don't think I am," she corrected herself. It had been ages since she'd been out on a date and even longer since she'd been in a relationship. And if she were being completely honest, she'd never felt as comfortable with any of her former boyfriends as she did after knowing Josiah just one day.

How bizarre was that?

Once all of the food was put away, Melanie walked into the guest bedroom, which she decided to use as her office and forced herself to sit down at the student desk in there with her laptop. It was time to push thoughts of Josiah aside for a little while and focus on trying to get some work done on her book.

Within minutes, her fingers began to fly. It was the first time in months that she felt her creativity coming back to her. In her mind, her characters were starting to take form. Her editor continually begged her to put her thoughts and plots and plans down on paper, but Melanie didn't work that way. She was more of a fly-by-the-seat-of-her-pants kind of girl— or a pantser. It worked for her.

When she finally stopped, she stretched and looked down at the corner of the computer screen and saw that almost two hours had gone by! And what was even better, she had almost five-thousand words done. Not a bad day's work! Taking a few minutes, she read over what she had written and couldn't suppress a smile—her hero bore a strong resemblance to her sexy next door neighbor. She wondered what he'd think of that.

With a chuckle, she stood and walked out to the kitchen to get herself something to drink. Thinking about the story she was creating, she knew it was too soon for her hero and heroine to kiss, but that didn't mean she didn't want them to.

And what was worse, she found she wanted to know what her very own hero, Josiah, kissed like.

It was almost five in the afternoon. She wasn't the least bit hungry but decided she was going to invite him over for dinner. Maybe she'd be hungry later. With a renewed sense of purpose, Melanie went into the bathroom to freshen up and then walked out to the living room and grabbed her jacket. With a steadying breath, she opened the door and walked out toward Josiah's house.

Feeling a little self-conscious, she tentatively knocked on the door. Was she being too obvious? Should she be playing a little hard to get? As soon as Josiah opened the door she had her answer.

No.

She didn't want to play hard to get.

She didn't want to play at all.

Well…sort of. A small smile tugged at her lips. "Hey," she said, her breath visible in the cold air.

"Hey. Come on in." Josiah stepped aside and once she was in, he closed the door. "So…what's up?"

Where did she even begin? Part of her simply wanted to pounce on him—to kiss him and be kissed by him—but she had a little more couth than that. "Um…I wanted to see if maybe you were free for dinner."

He smiled and Melanie felt her knees go weak. "Dinner, huh?"

She nodded.

"You didn't mention anything about it while we were grocery shopping."

Okay, so he wasn't going to make this easy for her. Fine. Two could play at this game. Stepping in close to him—very close—she met his gaze. "It wasn't on my mind then," she said, her voice low and just a little sultry. "After our little talk earlier, I decided that…dinner…might not be a bad idea."

She watched his expression turn serious as he swallowed hard and mentally high-fived herself.

"So…uh…sure," he said, his eyes locking on her lips. "Dinner sounds good."

Feeling a little wicked, she leaned in even closer until her body brushed his and then slowly moved away. "Good," she said. "That's good." A breathy little sigh escaped before she took a full step back. "So I'll see you at seven. Will that work for you?"

A muscle ticked in Josiah's jaw as he slowly shook his head. "No. No I don't think it will."

Her eyes widened slightly. "Oh?"

Lightning quick, Josiah reached out and grabbed her hand and gently tugged her against him. "What's going on here, Melanie?" he asked lowly.

She could have played dumb, but what was the point?

"Like I said, you gave me a lot to think about earlier. And I have. I thought we'd have dinner together and…see where it led." Her heart was hammering in her chest at her bold confession. This so wasn't like her and yet with Josiah, it seemed natural. Scary, but natural.

His expression was still serious as his eyes scanned her face. "What changed your mind?"

"It wasn't a matter of changing my mind, it was a matter of taking a step back and making sure we weren't making a mistake."

He quirked a dark brow at her. "And what makes you so sure we're not?"

She gave a slight shrug. "I'm still not sure. But I know I want to try." Swallowing, she moved against him. "We're on borrowed time here and I think we'd both regret it if we wasted time pretending to think about it."

"We?"

A low laugh was her first response. "Okay, me. I knew I'd regret it if I sat around pretending to think about it. I know it's only been twenty-four hours but it's all I've thought about. I could stand here and play the 'I don't really know you' game, but you took me all around town today and everywhere we went, people knew you. Everyone talked to you. Hell, it's like you have your own fan club around here so it's not like I can't trust you since obviously everyone does."

"I wouldn't call them a fan club. Not exactly…"

And just like that, the tension between them was broken. "Oh please…I was beginning to think they all had t-shirts with your picture on it. Maybe there was a parade in your honor during one of those ridiculous Christmas festivals."

He joined in her teasing. "It's not a particularly huge parade…normally me just driving down Main Street waving to people."

"Does the high school marching band follow you?"

"Only on Saturdays."

Melanie rested her head against his chest as she laughed. She could feel him laughing with her, felt his arms band around her waist as he slowly pulled her against him. When she lifted her head and looked up at his face, humor was suddenly the last thing on her mind. His name was a whisper on her lips.

"As much as I love talking with you and laughing with you, Melanie, right now all I really want is to kiss you."

Her hands skimmed up his chest and up and over his shoulders. "So what are you waiting for?" And much to her surprise, Josiah didn't move. The confusion she felt surely must have been obvious on her face.

With his forehead gently touching hers, he sighed. "I can't believe I'm saying this but…"

"But…?"

"I don't think we should do this."

"Oh." Melanie felt like she had been kicked in the gut and she wished the floor would just open up and swallow her. She was mortified. She'd never been the aggressor in a relationship and on her first time out of the gate she was shot down.

Dammit.

Not wanting to let him see how his words affected her, she carefully tried to disengage from his arms. When she realized he wasn't letting her go, she looked at him questioningly.

"I meant right now," he said quickly. "I just…I think if I kissed you right now, I wouldn't be content to let it stop here."

"I…I don't understand," she said quietly.

"If we kissed right now, Melanie, I would want to keep kissing you. We wouldn't talk. We wouldn't discuss it. Hell, we wouldn't have dinner." He motioned over his shoulder toward the ladder that led to his sleeping loft. "And it would be awkward as hell climbing the ladder the way I'm feeling right now."

"Oh," she sighed with a small smile. "But you were the one who…"

"I know. I know." This time it was Josiah who moved away. "So…I think we should stick to our original plan of meeting for dinner."

The sheepish look on his face was enough to melt her heart. "Okay then." Taking her own step away, she moved toward the door—not that it was far to move since the space was so small. "Then I'll plan on seeing you in a little bit."

He nodded. "Should I bring anything? Wine? Dessert?"

Opening the door, Melanie chuckled. "Just yourself. I think everything else is covered. It just won't be very gourmet. I sort of thought of this after we shopped."

"I'm not looking for a gourmet dinner, Melanie. I'm just looking to spend some time with you."

Unable to speak because she suddenly felt very emotional, she simply nodded and walked out the door, closing it softly behind her.

Chapter Four

Josiah walked to the kitchen to pour them each another glass of wine and saw it was after eleven. Where had the time gone? They'd eaten dinner and done nothing but talk for hours. In all his life he never remembered having a date—or dating anyone—where they never seemed to have an awkward silence.

Returning to the living room where Melanie was sitting on the sofa, he walked toward her and put their glasses on the coffee table.

"So I was thinking," she began, "we already know you're going to buy this place when I leave. So if you're ready, I don't see why you couldn't start doing stuff now." Reaching for her glass, she looked at him. "I could contact the attorney and start having the papers drawn up so you know I'm serious."

"I didn't think you were lying to me, Melanie," he said softly. "Are you really so sure you're going to go back to Raleigh at the end of those three months?"

She nodded. "My life is back there. I own a home—well, a condo—there. My dad is there. It's been just the two of us since my mom left. I couldn't just leave him."

Josiah reached over and took one of her hands in his. "You don't have to talk to me about this if you don't want to, but I…I'd like to hear about your family."

She sighed. "There's not much to tell. My mom left and my grandmother disowned us. That just left my dad and me." She shrugged. "End of story."

He gave her a disapproving look and she slowly pulled her hand away and sagged against the sofa cushions.

"Okay, fine," she moaned and then shifted to get more comfortable. "I don't think my mom ever wanted to be married. She and my dad dated all through high school, did the whole high-school-sweetheart thing and then she got pregnant with me. They got married but…I don't know. From what I remember and from the things my dad has shared with me over the years, she was never happy. She had big plans for her life after high school, like traveling and college, and because of me she couldn't do them."

"I'm sure she didn't blame you…"

Melanie shook her head. "No, but she did blame my dad. They fought all the time. Looking back he says he should have seen all the signs she was going to leave, but he didn't. Anyway, three days before Christmas, when I was five, she told my dad she was going out to buy my Christmas presents. They were kind of poor and lived paycheck to paycheck and so it was the first time they had the money for her to go shopping." Lowering her gaze from his, she stared into her wine glass. "She left with the money and never came back."

Josiah was speechless. He'd heard stories like this happening throughout his life, but never to someone he knew. His heart broke for the little girl she had been, wondering where her mother had gone. "Have you seen her since?"

She shook her head again. "Dad was a mess. I don't remember a lot of it, but I can remember him just sitting on the couch and crying. He was devastated. I was pretty self-sufficient for a five year old and I did my best to try and take care of him. We didn't celebrate Christmas that year."

He nodded with understanding. "Was Carol still in your life at that point?"

"Not much," she admitted. "You see, she wasn't happy that my parents had gotten married. She'd had big plans for my dad too and resented the fact he opted for a wife and child over college and a career. So it was really just the two of us."

"What about your mom's family? Where were they?"

"She was a late-in-life baby and her parents passed away when I was an infant. She was an only child just like my dad." She took a sip of her wine. "You know, as an adult I can see how they had everything against them—they were too young and didn't have a supportive family around them. But it doesn't make it any less painful to know…" Her voice began to tremble. "To know I was a contributing factor and so many people were just able to ignore me or walk away."

"Oh, Mel," he sighed and pulled her into his arms. "You shouldn't feel that way."

"How can I not?" she asked. "My mom was able to just walk away from me. I was her own child and it didn't seem to matter. And my grandmother never bothered to get to know me. And…and now here I am in her house, a place she specifically left to me, and I don't see it as a gift or a blessing. It's a reminder. It's nothing but a lousy reminder of her. It's like being stuck in a prison cell for three months."

Part of him wanted to take offense to her words, but he knew exactly what she meant. This wasn't about him and he couldn't make it be that way. She was carrying a lot of emotional baggage with her and maybe this was the first time she'd ever started to let it out.

"Can I ask you something?" he asked softly, placing a kiss on the top of her head. When she nodded, he pulled her a little more comfortably against him, tucking her against his side. "Why did you take the house then? If you felt this strongly about your feelings toward your grandmother and what this house represented, why come?"

"My dad talked me into it."

He waited for her to continue.

"He said it was a blessing in disguise. I was struggling with this book I'm supposed to be writing and he thought a forced change of scenery would help. The three months is about the time it usually takes for me to finish a book so the timeline would work. And it was specifically stipulated in the will how I had to stay for three months."

"It seems like an odd request."

She nodded. "I thought so too. And I have no idea why she would have put it in there since I didn't know her. Who knows what was going on in her head? She may have done it just to try to control me."

Josiah frowned. "Why would you say that?"

Pulling back a little, she looked up at him. "Are you sure you want to talk about this? I know you have good memories of her and I really don't want to ruin that for you. If she was nice to you, then those are the memories you deserve to keep, not the negative ones of my interactions with her."

He couldn't help but smile at her thoughtfulness and pulled her back so her head was on his shoulder. "I really want to know."

"About a month after my mom left, my grandmother showed up. Dad was still kind of a mess, the house was a disaster and I remember her coming in and just…she looked like she was sucking on a lemon." She shook her head. "She offered to help us out if we came to live with her."

Josiah couldn't really see an issue with that. It seemed exactly like the kind of thing Carol would do.

"But I would have to go away to school. She knew of some sort of private school or boarding school she wanted to send me to. Then she told Dad how she could get him a decent job and even knew the right girl for him."

Yikes.

"Dad threw her out. Every six months or so she would call and make the same offer, and every time he declined. After several years of this, they finally had a very, shall we say, heated argument about it. I remember I was washing the dinner dishes and the phone rang. Dad answered it and then went into his bedroom and shut the door. I didn't think the yelling would ever stop. When he came out, he looked at me and he looked sad, defeated. I asked him what was wrong and he said it was finally over—she wouldn't be bothering us anymore."

"I'm so sorry."

"I honestly didn't see why he was sad about it. She wasn't a very nice woman and all I could see was how we no longer had to deal with her calling and making us feel bad." She paused. "When I was older, in my early twenties, Dad and I talked about it. I finally asked him what had been said that day. He said she was making him choose—it was either me or a chance to have the life he deserved."

"Oh my God…"

She nodded. "She never saw me as a person. Never took the time to even try to see me as her granddaughter or to love me. I was something to get rid of. A reminder of a mistake my dad had made."

"I don't think he sees you that way."

"No, he never did and it bothered him when others did." She sighed. "That's what makes this all even more confusing. Why would she leave me anything in her will when she clearly hated and resented me? It doesn't make any sense."

"Maybe she came to realize she had made a mistake," Josiah suggested.

"I don't know. Maybe. Either way, here I am. Stuck in Christmastown. It's like a double whammy."

He chuckled. "Okay, I get the reason you feel the way you do about your grandmother, and I even understand why you might not love Christmas based on the story about your mom. But there has to be more to your dislike of Christmas than that."

"Dislike is a mild word."

He sat up fully and put some distance between them. "Come on…now I have to know."

"Fine, but after this we are done talking about me and my family. Maybe I'll put you under the microscope for a bit and see how you like it," she said with a half-hearted laugh.

"You could but it would be a very boring conversation. We were your typical American family with six kids. Money was always tight, we lived on a lot of hand-me-downs and ate a lot of macaroni and cheese because it was cheap. My parents are still happily married and all of my siblings, as I told you earlier, are doing well. I'm the beloved sheriff of this little town and happen to love my job." He sighed dramatically. "See? Boring."

"Does that mean I'm off the hook for the rest of my story?" she asked hopefully.

He shook his head and laughed. "Not a chance. Come on. Tell me why you hate Christmas. I'm thinking it's not all that bad."

When a slow, almost evil smile crossed her face, Josiah had a feeling he was about to majorly be proven wrong.

"We'll start with the Christmas Mom left."

"Naturally. And while horrible, I wouldn't think it would make you hold a lifelong grudge against Christmas."

"The following year Dad and I got the stomach flu. Bad. We spent days doing nothing but vomiting and praying for death."

He nodded. "Okay, that's pretty…gross, but still not enough not to get over."

"Dad got laid off the week before Christmas the next year."

He didn't even bother to stop her because now she was using her fingers to count all the ways she was proving her point.

"The next year was when he and my grandmother had that fight. It sort of took all the merry out of everything, knowing you were permanently disowned. But my favorite was the year we had gotten robbed the day before Christmas. By the time I was twelve, we both agreed to throw in the towel. Christmas was just not our thing and we simply quit fighting it and stopped celebrating. We've been very happy with our choice."

"So it's been…"

"A long time," she finished for him.

Knowing there was no way he was going to be able to find the right thing to say to her to change her mind, he decided to drop the subject. For now. But already his mind was reeling with ideas of how he could work on making her see Christmas in a new light. He could show her some positive aspects of it, and do his best to make this particular Christmas the best one ever.

"Okay then," he said and reached for his wine and finished it. "So how is the new book coming? Have you started on it?"

She shared with him how she had started seriously writing that afternoon and he loved how animated she got when she talked about her work. He normally read thrillers and mysteries, but her plans for a holiday romance sounded very nice.

"Now…wait a minute. If you're just writing it now, it won't be out for Christmas, will it?"

"The publishing world is very slow," she said. "This book won't come out until next October."

"Wow. That's a long time. Why so long?"

"By the time I hand in the finished manuscript it has to go through a first read, normally with an associate editor. Then they send it back to me with a round of edits, I send it back and then my editor reads it."

"Why doesn't she read it first? Wouldn't it save time?"

Melanie shook her head. "She needs to read a more polished version. It makes it easier for her to stay in the story rather than focusing on what needs to be changed."

He nodded.

"So she reads it and if she wants me to change anything, we do it. If she's good with it, it goes off to bookmaking where it will go through another two—sometimes three—rounds of edits to polish it and make sure there are no mistakes."

"Mistakes? It's fiction. How can there be mistakes?"

She chuckled and reached over to finish her own wine. "Grammatical mistakes. Sometimes I use a word or phrase too much or the way something is worded sounds awkward. That sort of thing. It's a very long process. And during all that, the cover needs to be designed and approved. Advanced copies go out to reviewers…it's a lot."

"I had no idea. It makes me appreciate books a little bit more. I never gave much thought to all the work that goes into them. I just figured the author wrote and then it got published."

"I wish!" she laughed. "The editing process can be very frustrating."

"I can only imagine," he said. "Well, if I wasn't already impressed with what you do, I definitely am now."

"Thank you," she said with a smile. Standing up, she picked up both of their glasses and took them to the kitchen. "So I set up my office in the guest room since there was a desk in there and I plan on buckling down and getting this story written. Now that I finally have a little direction, I think it's going to go smoothly."

"And you say a typical book takes you three months?"

She nodded. "Although, there have been one or two times when I was able to write a book in less than a month. There's no set schedule or rhyme or reason. I just write what the characters tell me."

"Interesting. So what if you finish this one before the end of the three months? Then what?"

"I'll send it in and start the editing process. The book isn't the only reason I'm here. It's just something that's going to help pass the time."

Walking across the room, Josiah came to the kitchen and slowly pinned her against the cabinets. "What about me?" he asked softly. "Is that what I am? A way to pass the time?"

She shook her head. "No, that's not what you are."

"That's good."

Before he knew it, she had her arms draped over his shoulders and was slowly pulling him in close. "You are a most unexpected surprise. And I still can't believe I've only been here two days."

"I know. I feel the same way."

"Do you have to work tomorrow?"

He nodded. "My schedule changes from week to week. Most of the time I try to keep it the same but my assistant had some family things to attend to so I try to be flexible. Was there something you wanted to do tomorrow?"

She shook her head again. "I was just curious about you. We spent a large part of the night talking about me. You know what my work schedule is like so I figured it might be nice to learn about the work habits of a sheriff. Maybe I can use that information in a future book," she teased.

"Very funny," he said and simply enjoyed the feel of her pressed against him. It was the oddest form of foreplay they had going on but he couldn't help but give in to it. "This particular sheriff goes into the office around eight in the morning and my day ends at five. I'm kind of a creature of habit—I come home, make myself something to eat and enjoy the peace and quiet of the land."

"I'll try to keep my loud music down for you," she said with a grin.

"I think we both know I'm not opposed to breaking in and putting a stop to it."

"Aha!" she cried. "You just admitted that you broke in!" She raised her hands in the air in a victory move. "Woo-hoo!"

He couldn't help but laugh. "I thought we weren't going to bring it up anymore."

"Technically, you brought it up first. I was merely commenting on your comment," she said saucily and wrapped her arms around him again. "I think it's only fair that I get to say something about it if you're going to talk about it."

Josiah rolled his eyes. He wanted to be annoyed but Melanie was so damn cute. Her eyes twinkled and her smile just made the entire room light up. Hugging her close, he debated on whether or not he should finally do what he'd been wanting to do since he first saw her.

Kiss her.

Slowly Melanie's smile faded and her expression turned thoughtful, serious. Maybe she was wondering if he was going to be the one to make the first move. Maybe since he had essentially put a stop to them doing it earlier she was a bit hesitant about it happening now. Normally Josiah was a confident man, a very confident man. And even though he knew with every fiber of his being that he wanted

Melanie—possibly more than he had ever wanted a woman—now that the time was here and he knew they were on the same page, he was nervous. There was something in the back of his mind whispering that maybe he was moving too fast or maybe he had built this attraction up in his mind simply because he had seen her naked before anything else.

All of which were valid points but it didn't stop Josiah from wanting her.

Melanie whispered his name and broke him out of his reverie. "I had a really good time with you today."

"Me too."

"I appreciate you spending your day off showing me around the town. That doesn't mean I'll remember where everything is, but it was nice to get a good look around just in case I need something and you're not around to help."

"I'm only a phone call away," he said.

"I can't rely on you for everything. Believe it or not I'm normally a very independent woman. I thrive on being self-sufficient."

He remembered her story earlier about how she was self-sufficient at the age of five and it felt like a fist squeezing his heart. When had someone taken care of her? He knew her father did the best he could, but it seemed like most of their lives had been one struggle after another. And he had a feeling Melanie took on much more responsibility than she ever should have had to.

"Well, I don't mind helping you," he said. "Actually, it's the sort of thing I thrive on."

"Yeah but…it goes with the whole sheriff thing, protect and serve and all that."

"Something like that," he said and shifted until they were touching from chest to toe. "Some I like to…protect and serve more than others."

She seemed to catch his meaning and smiled. "That's not very fair and impartial of you," she said softly and then seemed to purr at his touch.

"Maybe not. But it can't be helped. I'm not sure. It's all new to me."

Her eyes widened for just a second. "Protecting and serving?"

He shook his head. "The being impartial part. I'm finding I really have a strong desire to protect and take care of you."

Melanie released a shuttery breath and looked down at the floor. "Oh."

Reaching down, Josiah tucked a finger under her chin and gently nudged her to look at him. "Does that bother you?" he carefully asked.

"I don't know how to answer that," she replied honestly. "No one's ever…I mean other than my dad…no one's ever said that to me."

He couldn't help the grin that tugged at his lips. "That's good. I wouldn't want to compete with anyone."

"Believe me, Josiah. There's no competition."

That could be a good thing or a bad one, but he was opting for good right now. Her blue eyes studied him and as much as he knew he could probably stand here all night just looking at her, it was getting late and he could very easily make himself crazy staying inside his own head overthinking things.

Time for thinking—or overthinking—was over. Josiah cupped Melanie's face in his hands as he lowered his head toward hers. He almost stopped when he heard her whisper "Finally," but he just took it as all the encouragement he needed.

His lips brushed hers softly at first. He took one sip of her softness and then another before sinking in and truly getting a good taste. She hummed against him and it was a sexy sound that went right through him. Unable to hold back, his tongue teased at her lips and she opened for him. It was hot and wet and fairly consuming.

Josiah lost track of time and everything around them. He was completely lost in everything that was Melanie—the taste of her, the sounds she made and the feel of her pressed against him. It would be so easy for them to move the short distance to her bedroom but tonight wasn't the night for that. They needed more time. They needed to learn a little more about one another.

And he couldn't even believe he was talking himself out of what he so desperately wanted.

When they broke apart, both were gasping. He knew Melanie's heart was beating as wildly as his own because he could feel it, could see her pulse beating rapidly against the slender column of her throat.

When she said his name, he almost caved. Almost said to hell with good intentions and carried her into the other room.

But he didn't.

He saw the confusion on Melanie's face and knew he needed to explain. "I want you, Melanie, so much it scares me. But…I don't want us to rush. I know we talked about it earlier and I know we've only got three months, but that doesn't mean we have to jump into bed tonight." He sighed. "No matter how much I want to."

She smiled and seemed to visibly relax. "I know what you mean. I know what my body wants, but my head is talking pretty loudly to me right now."

"Yeah…mine too."

One soft hand cupped his cheek. "Thank you for being honest with me."

"Always," he said gruffly. "You never have to worry about that with me." Leaning forward, he kissed her one last time before forcing himself to stop. Slowly he turned away and headed for the front door.

"I better go. I have work in the morning." He turned and looked at her. "Can I see you tomorrow night?"

Wordlessly, she nodded.

"Good night, Melanie," he said and when she wished him one as well, he walked out and carefully closed the door behind him. And just as it had the previous night, the cold air was exactly what he needed.

He just wasn't sure how many more cold nights he could suffer through.

****

For two weeks it became their pattern—when Josiah worked, they'd have dinner together. It was always at Melanie's place because Josiah felt awkward about how small his place was, or so he said. Melanie knew he loved his place but it really wasn't great when they were both trying to maneuver in the kitchen. After one attempt, they opted to do all of their meals at her place, although they did alternate who cooked.

She was enjoying getting to know him and found that everything she learned only added to his appeal. One of the things she was trying to get him to change—and probably the only thing—was his lack of technology, specifically with music. The man still owned a CD player and that was the only way he listened to his music. When Melanie mentioned how much more efficient and space saving an iPod would be, he balked at it. He talked about the price and how he had such a great collection of music on CD, but she had a feeling it had more to do with changing the way he did things.

On Josiah's days off, Melanie took those days off as well and they would go out for lunch and he started showing her some of the towns surrounding Silver Bell. It still was a very different environment than what she was used to back in North Carolina, but she could see the charm to it. And at any other time of the year she probably would have felt the charm a little more herself.

Back home, she would have avoided all of the things she and Josiah were currently doing, the shopping and walking around town. He even took her ice skating twice! And maybe it was just her imagination but it seemed like everything was just…magnified here. The Christmas decorations, the music, the overall cheerfulness of the people were all over the top. At first she wanted to blame it solely on the town of Silver Bell itself, but even when they ventured to another town, she found it equally overwhelming.

Her writing was coming along better than she ever could have imagined and although Josiah kept asking her about the story, she was keeping it to herself. Normally she didn't share the details with anyone except her editor just because it was a habit, but now it was more because the couple she was writing about, bore a very strong resemblance to her and Josiah. The only difference was her fictional couple had already gotten hot and heavy with one another while she and Josiah were still…well, they were still *not* getting hot and heavy.

Sigh.

It wasn't for lack of desire or trying—at least on her part. Short of greeting him at the door naked, she wasn't sure what else she could do. The man was hell-bent on a slow seduction and it was getting harder and harder not to just blurt out how he didn't need to bother—she was a sure thing!

Maybe they could talk about it that night at dinner. His shift was slightly off so he wasn't going to get home until almost seven but maybe she could…

Her thoughts were interrupted by her cell phone ringing. Glancing down she saw it was her dad and she couldn't help the smile that spread across her face. "Hey, Dad!"

"Hey, sweetheart! How are you doing?"

"I'm doing great," she said and realized she really was.

"Really? That's wonderful! How's the book coming?"

She shared with him how fast things were coming to her, without telling him exactly why or who was making that possible. "You were totally right, Dad. I needed the change of scenery. It's really helped me a lot."

"I'm so glad, Mel. I really am." He paused. "So listen, Thanksgiving is next week and I was wondering if you wouldn't mind me coming up there to join you for it."

She gasped in surprise. "Do you mean it? You'd really come all the way up here?"

"Of course I would. Why wouldn't I?"

"We talked about this before I left. I know you're busy at work and it's a lot of traveling and the cost of flying is astronomical at the last minute. I don't want you spending all that money because of me."

He sighed. "Mel, it's been a long time since we've had to count pennies. Things are good. You know it and I know it. I know old habits die hard but the thought of not seeing you for Thanksgiving was really bringing me down. I miss you."

She felt tears brimming in her eyes. "Aw…I miss you too," she said, her voice trembling a little. "I just don't want to cause you any undue stress."

"You're not," he assured her. "I'm going to fly in Thursday morning—and yes it was the cheaper way to go—and then I'll be going home Friday night."

"But…but that's really quick. It seems like a lot of time and money for such a short visit."

"I don't look at it that way," he said. "You and I have never been apart for Thanksgiving and besides, there's a part of me that would really like to see the old cabin. I haven't been there since I was a kid." He paused. "Unless…unless you have plans."

Melanie couldn't help but smile at the sudden uncertainty in her father's voice. "Actually, I had planned on making a scaled down Thanksgiving dinner for me and…a friend."

"A friend, huh?" he asked, and she could hear the curiosity and excitement in his tone.

She groaned. "Ugh…okay. So I met someone when I got here. He's actually living on the property." She gave him the Reader's Digest version of her first meeting with Josiah—minus the naked in the tub part—and how they'd been spending time together.

"I can't believe you haven't mentioned this," he said and then sighed. "Why is the father always the last to know?"

She knew he was teasing her so she laughed. "Oh knock it off. I'm not a kid anymore and it's not like this is something serious. Josiah knows I'm leaving at the end of the three months and I plan on selling the property to him. He had tried to get your mother to sell it to him, but she never would."

"Well, I'm sure she had her reasons."

Melanie snorted with bit of annoyance. "More like her just trying to control things like she always did."

John sighed. "Look, let's not even think about it. I've got some work to finish up before I go so I'll just plan on seeing you Thursday morning, okay?"

"Absolutely. And Dad?"

"Yeah?"

"I'm really glad we're going to spend Thanksgiving together."

"Me too, sweetheart. Me too."

Later that night, after she and Josiah had finished dinner, she shared the news with him.

"I know we planned on just having a low-key dinner for the two of us, but…"

He reached over and squeezed her hand. "Melanie, you never have to apologize to me for wanting to spend time with your family. If I didn't have to work Thanksgiving Day, I'd probably be driving to spend the day with my brothers," he smiled at her. "And I would have brought you with me."

"I know…I just…it feels a little weird."

"Why?"

She shrugged. "He's coming here because it's a connection to his childhood. You have a lifelong connection to this place and my grandmother. And then there's the whole you and me thing and…"

"Wait a minute…are you afraid to tell your dad about us?" he asked and Melanie could see the hurt he was trying to hide.

"No, that's not it at all. I already mentioned it to him and he's excited to meet you."

"Okay, then what's the problem?"

She stood up and began clearing away the dinner dishes. "It's like there's this weird connection between all of us and then there's the fact that I've never had a boyfriend spend a holiday with us and…I can't explain it," she said with exasperation. "So basically this is all new territory and I feel awkward and stupid, like I'm a kid again!"

He stood up and came into the kitchen and wrapped his arms around her. "So I'm your boyfriend, huh?"

She playfully swatted him away and laughed. "Cut it out! I'm being serious here!"

He laughed and pulled her back against him when she moved away. "I am being serious!" he said. "It's just been a long time since anyone called me their boyfriend, that's all."

"Are you kidding me? I know you've dated. We've talked about it."

"Of course I've dated but…you know…I kind of feel a little old to be somebody's boyfriend."

That made Melanie laugh harder. "So what am I supposed to call you? My male friend? My make-out buddy? What are my options?"

He hugged her tightly and then released her. "I don't think I'm particularly fond of any of those."

"Got any better ones?" she asked, but her back was to him. She smiled when she felt him press up from behind her and begin to nuzzle her neck.

"I would say lover but we haven't crossed that bridge yet," he said softly between kisses.

"And whose fault is that?"

He chuckled and his breath tickled her skin. "I want to make sure you don't have any regrets."

Turning off the water, Melanie turned in his arms. "I think we've already covered that too. No regrets. Not with you." Leaning forward, she kissed him gently on the lips and felt her heart skip a beat when Josiah took control of it. She loved that about him— his passion and the way he always made her feel. She knew that should they ever move forward in this relationship and get physical, it would be incredible.

Josiah slowly broke the kiss and lifted his head. "So what are you saying?" he teased. "That maybe we should take this inside?"

She almost wept with relief. *Finally!* It was on the tip of her tongue to say it but when she met his gaze and saw all of the heat and need there, she was suddenly overwhelmed and humbled by it. Rather than speak, she nodded and took him by the hand and led the way. Melanie only made it a few feet when he stopped her.

"I wasn't pushing, you know that right?"

Something inside of her snapped. Turning toward him, she angrily put her hands on her hips. "Let me ask you something…do you want me? I mean do you even *want* to have sex with me?"

Josiah looked at her with something akin to shock. "Are you serious? How can you even ask me that?"

"Because every time I think we're going to move in this direction it's like you try to talk me out of it. I know you're not rushing me. I know you haven't rushed me. But you know what? Right now? I'm going to rush you!" And with that she stood behind him and literally shoved him toward her bedroom door.

When they were both in the bedroom, she closed the door behind her and leaned against it. Josiah turned to her and smiled. "And here I was trying to be a gentleman…"

Slowly Melanie walked toward him until they were toe to toe. "And I love that about you, but every night when you leave here I go a little more insane. You kiss me and turn me inside out and then you're just able to get up and go."

He shook his head. "It's not that easy; believe me."

"Then why? If this isn't what you want or if you're having second thoughts, just tell me!"

Carefully, he put his arms around her waist. "I really was trying not to rush you. I guess I didn't realize you were just as anxious as me."

"Well I am," she said with a pout.

"What can I do to prove to you how much I want you?" he whispered huskily, his hands already beginning to roam from her waist to her shoulders and down her arms.

"Hmm…" she purred. "Maybe you could kiss me again."

He did. "And what else?"

Melanie pulled her shirt up and over her head. "And maybe you can touch me…here." She placed her hands over her breasts. "While you kiss me."

He did.

And then Melanie didn't have to say anything else.

Josiah knew exactly how to prove to her how much he wanted her. And he did. All night long.

Chapter Five

"So there we were, marching down Main Street as part of the parade and the snow was falling down at such a rate that we couldn't even see the people standing on the sidewalks!" John said, unable to control the laughter. "And I don't know which was worse—the fact that we were still out there marching or that people were standing there watching!"

Josiah and Melanie laughed with him. They had just finished their Thanksgiving dinner and John was sharing some of his memories of his time in Silver Bell.

"We've had quite a few events like that," Josiah said. "The people here are die-hard fans of a parade and festival and we're so used to the snowy weather that it doesn't really stop us."

Relaxing back in his seat, John smiled. "We don't get a whole heck of a lot of snow in Raleigh. Back in 2000 we got two feet of it but that's the worst I can remember. Not that I miss it, but sometimes it was a lot of fun to just go outside and play in it."

"Well then maybe you should come back next month," Melanie said. "If you can get the time off."

John shrugged. "I don't know. Maybe. I'd hate to make the trip and then not be able to get back home when I need to leave."

Both Melanie and Josiah nodded. "Okay, you two boys sit and relax while I clean up," Melanie said as she stood.

"Nonsense," John said. "You cooked so we can certainly help you clean up."

She held up a hand to stop him. "The kitchen is too small for the three of us. Besides, you were interested in seeing the inside of Josiah's place. Why don't you go and do that? I've got this covered."

John looked over at Josiah. "Would you mind?"

Actually, Josiah was thrilled at the prospect. Ever since Melanie had mentioned how her father was coming to visit, he had been trying to come up with a way to get the man alone so he could talk to him about a couple of things. "Not at all," he finally answered and then turned to Melanie. "Are you sure you don't mind? There's kind of a big mess in there."

She waved him off. "And I have a system so I'd prefer to do it alone. Go. Dessert won't be for quite a while so there's no rush."

Smiling, Josiah walked over and kissed her and felt her stiffen for a minute before she relaxed. He guessed it was because her father was standing five feet away but he didn't care. They were adults and they were finally lovers. Besides, he didn't think John Harper had a problem with them showing a little bit of affection.

"Come on, John," Josiah said as he stepped away from Melanie. "But be warned, it really is tiny."

"I'm so intrigued by the concept," John said, pulling on his coat. "I keep seeing these things on all the DIY shows and even at the local home shows but I've never gone in one." The two men walked to the front door and then out. Out on the front porch, the cold air had them both hissing in a breath. "I'll tell you what, I really don't miss this weather."

Josiah chuckled. "It's not so bad. I don't know anything else but this. But I can tell you, it certainly wakes you up as soon as you step outside."

"I remember."

They walked across the yard and Josiah opened the door and motioned for John to go in first. He remembered the first time he had shown Melanie his place and how nervous he'd been. With John, however, he was feeling a sense of pride at showing off his little place. And beyond that, he was a little nervous about the conversation he was about to start.

"Wow," John said, stepping inside. "This really is something. I mean…it's small, no doubt about it. But everything's functional. There's no spot that isn't multi-functioning."

"Everything has a purpose," Josiah said. "It does make you live a minimalist lifestyle and I'll admit I do have a lot of stuff in storage, but this was a short-term solution to getting things in order."

"So you really thought my mother was going to sell you the place, huh?"

Josiah shrugged. "I had hoped. I thought we were well on the way to doing that when she allowed me to put this place on the property. I never expected…" He cleared his throat. "I mean, her death was unexpected."

John nodded but kept moving around the space. "From what her lawyer was able to tell me, she wasn't ill. She died peacefully in her sleep."

"I'm very sorry for your loss. Melanie explained to me that you had been estranged but…"

"She was still my mother," John finished for him and turned to sit on the sofa. "She had a stubborn streak and she thought she knew what was best for everyone." There was no bitterness in his voice, only sadness. "I think if she had only listened once in a while rather than wanting to be heard, things could have been different." He sighed and then shook his head. "Anyway, Mel tells me the people here in Silver Bell had a much better relationship with my mother."

Nodding, Josiah pulled his lone barstool away from the breakfast nook and sat down. "Yeah, I think it was a bit of a shock for her the first few times she met people around here, but now she's used to it. Everyone in town loves her."

John looked at him curiously. "My mother or Melanie?"

Josiah chuckled. "Both, but I was referring to Melanie. I think the first time we went into town and talked with people who knew Carol she was a little taken aback." He smiled at the memory. "But she didn't correct them or tell them they were wrong about Carol, she accepted their condolences gracefully."

John gave a small smile. "That's my girl. I always regretted the way things happened for her. I did my best but…"

Here was the opening Josiah was hoping for. "She's shared a lot of her past with me," he said carefully.

John let out another sigh and wiped a weary hand down his face. "Her life certainly hasn't been easy and I take a lot of the blame for that."

Josiah looked at him oddly. "Why? It seems to me you're the only one who gave a damn. You stuck it out and took care of her, like a good parent should. Why would you even blame yourself?"

"It's hard to explain but…her mom and I were just too young. We never should have gotten married."

"That wouldn't have changed anything for Melanie. And you were just as young as her mom and yet you stepped up to the plate and were responsible. She's lucky to have you."

When John looked over at him, he had tears in his eyes. "Thank you for saying that. I just wish…I wish things could have been different for her. She has so many bad memories of her time growing up and most of them are because I failed in some way."

Josiah shook his head firmly. "That's not true. You did the best you could. It seems other people failed the both of you." He paused. "Have you ever…" He stopped and thought about how to word his question. "What I mean is, in all these years, has Melanie's mother ever reached out to you?"

John shook his head sadly. "I'm not sure if I'm happy or mad about it. I hate that Mel grew up without a mom, but I think it could have been worse if she'd come back at some point and then left again."

"I can understand that." He sighed and looked around and then decided to get to the heart of what he really wanted to talk about. "So…about Christmas."

John looked up at him and let out a mirthless laugh. "Yeah. Christmas," he sighed. "I'm sure you think it's a little odd."

There was no way he could honestly deny it so he didn't even try. "I have to admit, I was a little shocked when she first starting talking about it. Then she explained why she felt the way she did and I could understand it. Sort of."

"I always hoped we could overcome it, but if something bad is going to happen, it happens at Christmas."

"Surely there are some good memories? Something, somewhere that was positive? My family didn't have a lot of money when we were growing up—there were six of us kids—but just because we didn't get a lot of presents didn't make it bad. Did you have any traditions that Melanie enjoyed?"

John studied him carefully for a long moment—almost to the point of it feeling awkward—before he spoke. "She probably would never admit it, but she loves sugar cookies. We used to bake them when she was small – before her mom left. I'm not much of a baker so when I tried making them with her it was with refrigerated cookie dough," he chuckled. "But even when we don't celebrate Christmas, she always seems to have sugar cookies in the house. And she loves having them with cocoa."

"That's a nice memory," he said. "I'd like to help her make some new ones."

John's eyes narrowed slightly. "You know she's only here for the three months, right?"

Josiah nodded. "It doesn't matter how long she's here for. She'll be here for Christmas this year and I want to do something to make it special for her."

"What about you? Don't you have family of your own to spend it with?"

"Normally I do. But this is something really important to me, John. If I only get to have one Christmas with your daughter, I want it to be the kind where, years from now, she'll look back and have a good memory of it."

And then John seemed to relax and the look he gave Josiah told him he completely understood exactly how strongly he felt for Melanie. "I like the fact that if I'm not here to spend Christmas with her, you are."

That made Josiah smile. "I thought the two of you don't spend Christmas together?"

"We spend the day together, we just don't celebrate."

With a nod, Josiah stood and walked over to the refrigerator to grab them something to drink. "You're welcome to celebrate it with us this year," he said. "I'm hoping to make it the best one yet for her."

"Son, if you can do that, I'm here to help in any way I can."

****

Melanie was still a little teary-eyed the following week when she thought about her dad. She had thought she was okay with temporarily living so far away from him, but after his short Thanksgiving visit, she realized just how much she missed him. Josiah must have noticed because he took her out on a proper date—out to dinner, a movie and dessert.

When they got back to the cabin, he didn't even ask if he could stay. They walked in the door and he helped her take her coat off before shedding his own and then took her by the hand and led her to the bedroom.

It scared her a little at how well Josiah seemed to know her and could so easily read her wants, her needs, her moods, but right now in this very moment, she was grateful for it. He kissed her as he undressed her and when they crawled into bed together, Melanie closed her eyes and sighed at how perfect it felt.

Every touch, every kiss, every movement not only showed her how much Josiah cared for her, but it was making it hard to ignore how much he was coming to mean to her as well.

And much later, when they both should have been asleep, she wrapped herself around him and placed her head on his shoulder, her hand over his heart—it was still beating rapidly after all they had shared.

"Thank you," she whispered.

He kissed the top of her head. "For what?"

"For the perfect night."

She could feel him smiling. "I aim to please," he said lightly.

With a chuckle, Melanie lifted her head and looked at him. "I wasn't just talking about what we just did in here."

He gave her a lopsided grin. "Neither was I."

"Somehow I doubt that," she teased and then relaxed back against him. "I feel like I've been in a funk for the last few days and it was nice to get out of the house and have such a good night. That restaurant was fantastic. We'll have to go there again."

"Any time you want," he said and hugged her a little closer. "I hate that I have to work tomorrow."

"Why?"

"Because I'm enjoying this—holding you in my arms, both of us a little sleepy and relaxed after making love and just talking about our day."

She frowned. "And that's going to make going to work bad?"

He nodded. "I could stay like this all night with you, Melanie. But I know I've got to get some sleep if I'm going to be at all useful in the morning."

"You work too hard, Sheriff Stone," she said, placing a kiss on his chest. "Do you ever get vacation time?"

"Oh yeah," he said and then yawned. "A couple of weeks throughout the year. Why? Want to go someplace tropical with me?"

She chuckled. "I was just thinking it might be nice for you to come to Raleigh and see where I live." As soon as the words were out of her mouth she felt him stiffen slightly. "It's not as festive as Silver Bell," she added quickly, "but there are a lot of great places to see and some wonderful restaurants."

Josiah stayed silent until Melanie lifted her head again to look at him. "What?" she asked softly. "What's the matter?"

Reaching out, he cupped her cheek in his hand. "I don't want to think about a time when you're back there and I'm still here."

Everything in her softened against him. "Oh…"

Slowly, as if giving her time to stop him, Josiah rolled them over until she was nestled beneath him. Then he kissed her, slowly. Thoroughly. Melanie knew it was partially a distraction method, but she didn't care. She loved kissing him and poured everything she had into kissing him back.

Her heart began to race as his hand roamed from her shoulder down to her knee and back again. She couldn't help but arch into him. And as he loved her slowly for the second time that evening, she had to wonder how she was going to survive the time when he was here and she was back at home. Because no matter how hard she tried to convince herself she was okay with this being a short-term relationship, her heart was getting more and more involved.

And it wasn't just because she was someplace new and he was keeping her company and it wasn't simply because of proximity. Melanie knew it would take very little effort for her to completely go over the edge and fall hopelessly and completely in love with Josiah Stone. Maybe she was there already and was just refusing to admit it.

He whispered her name between kisses in that deep timbered voice of his and it sent shivers down her spine—in a good way. The urge to tell him exactly how she was feeling was so strong, it was almost overwhelming. But she knew now wasn't the time. She was too caught up in all of the things he was making her feel.

And as he took her over the edge and she cried out his name, she met his gaze and saw mirrored there everything she was feeling.

One day soon, she wasn't going to be able to hold it back.

One day soon, she was going to have to tell him exactly how she felt.

And one day soon, she was going to have to figure out how it was she was supposed to say goodbye.

****

This was the time of year Josiah loved most of all. He loved the festivals, the parades and the overall excitement that seemed to be everywhere. But this was the first year he was feeling some of that excitement for himself. John Harper had been extremely helpful in giving him ideas to possibly warm Melanie up towards Christmas and he was having a hard time patiently waiting to find out for himself.

He had a lot of responsibilities right now, more so than usual. His days were longer and as much as he was enjoying it all, there was a sense of annoyance because it was keeping him away from Melanie more and more.

Silver Bell's official Christmas parade was this upcoming weekend and Josiah had been casually dropping hints that he wanted Melanie to go. So far she had yet to offer and he wasn't sure what he could do other than handcuff her and put her in the back of his cruiser.

The image brought a smile to his face and he made a mental note to see how she felt about handcuffs in other scenarios.

Pushing that sexy thought aside, Josiah did his best to go over his checklist for his staff regarding their parade responsibilities. The weather forecast showed it was going to be cold—but that was the norm—and a chance of flurries. The snow always made people a little more excitable than usual and he almost hoped the weather would hold off until the end of the parade.

Next he drove the parade route and saw that all of the businesses along it had already decorated and that the sidewalks were cleared and ready for spectators. Afterwards, he went to the high school and gave his annual speech to the students and faculty who would be participating in the parade to go over their schedule and rules of conduct.

By the time he was back at his office, he was mentally exhausted and wanted nothing more than to be at home with Melanie in front of a fire. Hmmm…he thought. Maybe he'd pick up the ingredients for s'mores and they could make them in front of the living room fire. And that's when yet another image of Melanie popped into his mind. In this one he was licking chocolate from her lips and sweet marshmallow from her fingers.

He groaned. If he didn't stop fantasizing about her like this while at work, people were going to notice. When his phone rang, he was grateful for the distraction. "Sheriff's office," he said as he answered the phone.

"You'd think with such a lofty position you'd have a secretary answering the phone for you," came his brother Mark's taunt.

Josiah laughed. "Not all of us are prima donnas," he said. "What's going on? Aren't you supposed to be doing something tech-related to make the world a better place right about now?"

"Ha, ha, very funny," Mark said. "I wanted to call and see if you were still set on staying put in Silver Bell for Christmas. Lisa wanted me to ask because she's trying to finalize her menu. She and Kelly are splitting cooking responsibilities this year."

"Yeah, I'm staying put this year."

"You got roped into working? You know you're the boss, right? You can demand someone else cover the time," Mark said with his authoritive big-brother tone.

"No it's not that," he began awkwardly. "It's…well…I…"

"Oh for the love of it, Josiah, just spit it out! If you don't want to come, you can just say it. I'm not going to hold it against you or anything. I know it's a bit chaotic with all the kids and whatnot. I completely understand."

"I met someone," he blurted out.

Mark was silent for a minute.

"Mark? You still there?"

"I am," he said, his voice a little thoughtful. "So…who is she? A local girl?"

Josiah told him all about Melanie and her connection to Silver Bell. "We've been spending a lot of time together and she's really got a hang up about Christmas and I just want to spend it with her and show her it doesn't have to be bad." He went on to tell him about Melanie's history with the holiday and his plans for her this year.

"Dude, I know you think you're awesome and all, but one Christmas with you is not going to wipe out a lifetime of bad ones."

"I know that," Josiah snapped.

"Do you? Because I'd hate to see you get your hopes up like you're going to be the one to change everything around for her and when it doesn't work out that way, you're going to be all butt-hurt and pout."

"I don't pout."

"You are the king of pouting," Mark deadpanned. "I can tell you're pouting right now."

Josiah was ready to deny it but knew he wouldn't be able to pull it off. "Anyway…"

"Anyway, "Mark interrupted, "I think it's great you met someone and you want to do something this big for her. Just…be careful, especially since she's not planning on staying in Silver Bell then…" He paused. "Oh…that's what you're hoping for. You're hoping you'll make this grand gesture and she'll want to stay."

He sighed with frustration. "Am I hoping for that? Yes. Am I counting on it?" He paused. "I don't know. I have no idea how she's going to respond to any of this. I haven't even been able to convince her to come to the damn parade. Every time we go someplace and she hears Christmas music, she just about loses her mind."

"Then you definitely have your work cut out for you. If she feels that strongly about the whole thing, I can't imagine her wanting to live there full-time. That town has Christmas written all over it—and not just in December. It's a year-round thing there, dude. Have you even thought about that?"

"Of course I have! I just hoped…I guess I want her to stay for me and not have it be about the damn town."

"If it were any other town in the country, I think you'd have a shot. But Silver Bell? For someone who hates Christmas? You really are asking for a miracle."

"Perfect time of year for one!" Josiah quipped.

He heard Mark chuckle. "Josiah, I want you to think really hard about this. What are you going to do if this effort of yours…if it isn't enough? What happens if she still wants to leave? What are you going to do?"

It was something Josiah was refusing to let himself about. In his mind, Melanie was going to stay. She was going to realize she was in love with him and that they were meant to be together.

And learn to love Christmas again.

"I can't think about that," he replied honestly. "Mark...you're going to have to trust me on this one. I've never felt like this before and I'm willing to do whatever it takes to show Melanie how much she means to me."

On the other end, Mark sighed. "I'm not going to talk you out of this, am I?"

"Afraid not. This is something I have to do."

"Promise me something and then I've got to get back to work."

"Anything."

"If things don't go quite the way you planned, promise me you'll come here for a few days and hang out with us. I don't want you staying up there alone."

Josiah felt like his brother had reached into his chest and squeezed his heart. He had to swallow the lump in his throat before he could answer. "I will," he finally said.

When he hung up, Josiah leaned back in his chair, let out a shaky breath and scrubbed a weary hand over his face.

A knock on his office door was the only thing stopping him from obsessing about the conversation with his brother. "Come in." He looked up to see Betty Jo Taylor, the head of the parade committee, standing in the doorway. "What can I do for you today, Ms. Taylor?" he asked pleasantly.

She was a short and plump woman in her sixties and Josiah towered over her. Wringing her hands, she looked up at him with tears in her eyes. "It's terrible, Sheriff, just terrible!"

Before he asked what she was referring to, he led her over to a chair and helped her sit down. "Okay now, why don't you tell me what's going on?" he asked gently.

"Well, you know how we always try to get a small-town celebrity to participate in the parade, right?"

He nodded.

"I had worked for months to get the channel seven weathergirl, Susannah Kane, to come and join us. We had everything all set and she just called and backed out!" she cried. "She didn't even give us a reason. She just said she couldn't do it!"

Josiah wasn't sure what he was supposed to do with this information so he waited Betty Jo out.

Wiping at the tears that had yet to really fall, she looked up at Josiah full of hope. "I know you've been dating Carol Harper's granddaughter—she's an author, right?"

A knot instantly formed in his stomach when he realized where Betty Jo was going with this. All he could do was nod.

"I know it's short notice and all but…do you think Melanie would do it? All she'd have to do is ride in the back of Ed Kincaid's red convertible and wave," she said, her voice getting more and more cheerful as she spoke. "I figured we could set up a display of her books in the library and maybe get her publisher to ship some to us by priority mail so we can set up a table for her to sign them after the parade! Can you ask her, Josiah?"

His eyes went wide. "Me? You want me to ask Melanie?"

Betty Jo stood and fluffed her hair. "Well of course you," she said with a chuckle. "How could she say no to such a handsome man?" She reached up and patted him on the cheek. "You know how much her grandma loved Silver Bell and all the Christmas festivities. I think it would be real sweet to have her granddaughter here to fill in for her! The townspeople will go nuts! And just think of the story we can write for the paper!" She let out a little squeal of delight. "You ask her, Sheriff, and give her my number!"

In the blink of an eye, Betty Jo was gone and Josiah felt like he had just been through a tiny tornado.

He was having a hard enough time getting Melanie to give him an answer about just coming to watch the damn parade. How was he supposed to convince her to be a part of it?

****

Melanie froze in place with the butcher knife precariously close to cutting her finger. She stared at Josiah as if he had grown a second head. "You told her no, right?"

"Well…"

"Why couldn't you just tell her no?" she cried. "You know how I feel about these things!" Tossing the knife down, she paced back and forth in the kitchen. "And you honestly think I'd want to sit in a red car—probably wearing a Santa hat or something—and wave to the crowds while Christmas music is playing all around me? Seriously?"

"Okay, I'll admit I didn't think it through, but it all happened so fast!" He explained to her how Betty Jo was. "And I thought she was going to cry! What was I supposed to do?"

"Um…say no," she said sarcastically.

Josiah crossed the room and went to her and wrapped her in his arms. She fought him at first, but after a minute she sagged against him with her head on his chest. "I've gotta be honest with you here, Mel," he said lightly and hoped she didn't mind him using her nickname. "I don't see what the big deal is. They're willing to make a fuss over you and your books, which your publisher will love. You just have to smile and wave. If you want, you can put your iPod on and we'll hide the earbuds so you won't have to hear the Christmas music. Come on. What do you say?"

She sighed loudly. "And you won't let them force me to wear a Santa hat, right?"

He couldn't help but chuckle as he hugged her close and kissed the top of her head. "If you'd like, we'll get you a special tiara or one of those really furry hats."

"I wouldn't mind the tiara," she said, but she was still muffled against his chest.

"Then I'll see what I can do," he promised.

When she pulled away and went back to making dinner, Josiah felt a wave of relief wash over him. She was coming to the parade. Granted, it was still under protest, but he couldn't imagine her not getting caught up in all the fun.

Looking at her now, he was a little overwhelmed with emotion. Her whole life was upside down right now and yet she was rolling along with it. It was one of the things he loved about her.

Wait. Love?

Yeah. No doubt about it.

Slowly, Josiah walked over to her and carefully took the knife from her hand and put it aside. When she looked up at him questioningly, he cupped her face in his hands and kissed her. Slowly, softly at first, and then he went deeper. She didn't shy away from meeting his passion and when he maneuvered them out of the kitchen and toward the bedroom, she went willingly.

And when he closed the door behind him and slowly undressed her, she gave him a sexy smile and returned the favor.

They didn't need to talk about it.

They didn't need to think about anything beyond this moment.

And right now, this moment—in Josiah's mind—was the most perfect one yet.

****

Two days later, she found him sitting on the front steps of his tiny house frowning. Pulling her coat tightly around her, she walked over. "Are you okay?"

For a minute, it didn't seem like he'd heard her and then he looked up. "You know how sometimes something seems like a really good idea but then you realize you didn't really think it through?"

She felt a wave of panic for a moment, fearing he was referring to them and their relationship. Instead of speaking, she simply nodded.

"Yeah, well…I was all about downsizing and saving money so I could buy this property, that I didn't realize how much I was giving up by living in such a small space."

She sat down beside him – which wasn't easy considering how narrow the steps were. "Like what?"

Turning his head, he looked at her for a minute and then turned away. "You know what? It's nothing," he said dismissively. "It's not a big deal." He stood up quickly and held out his hand to her. "What would you like to do today? How about we go to lunch at that sandwich shop you like so much?"

Melanie knew he was trying to change the subject, but she wasn't about to let that happen. "I don't want to go out to lunch. I want you to tell me what's bothering you."

He frowned at her. "I already told you it's nothing."

She rolled her eyes. "Seriously? You make me tell you everything. I share all of my stupid feelings with you and you're not willing to do the same?"

His shoulders sagged and he sighed. "Okay, but once I tell you, you can't complain that you didn't really want to know."

"I wouldn't do that."

The look of disbelief he gave her spoke volumes.

"Josiah…" she whined.

"Fine," he growled and took a few steps away and began to pace. "I picked this place because it had everything I needed. I was able to declutter and get rid of a lot of stuff I didn't need and it seemed perfect. I still have a storage unit because I knew I wasn't going to live here forever."

"O-kay," she said slowly.

"Anyway…" He sighed and stopped pacing to look at her. "Don't laugh but…I miss having my Christmas decorations up."

Melanie wasn't sure what she was expecting him to say, but that wasn't it. "That's it? That's what has you all sad and mopey?"

"Mopey?" he repeated incredulously. "I am not mopey."

"Sweetheart, you are the poster-child for mopey right now." She walked over and hugged him. "Okay, so why can't you decorate?"

He pulled back and looked down at her and the frown was back. "You've seen the inside of my place right?"

She nodded.

"There's no room for a tree or a manger or…anything!"

"Well maybe not all those things but I'm sure you can do a few of them," she said. "You can hang a stocking and maybe some twinkly lights."

He shook his head. "I know you don't get it but…" He shrugged. "I like having a tree. I like decorating it and seeing gifts under it."

"You have one at the office, right?"

Releasing her, he moved away. "Just…let's just forget about it." He fished his car keys out of his pocket. "Come on. Let's go into town and grab something to eat."

She knew he was smiling but that it wasn't genuine. While she might not understand what all the fuss was about, it was clearly a big deal to him. "Let me just go and grab my stuff," she said and walked back into the cabin. A quick glance around showed her it was pretty sparse inside. It was decorated but not in anything from this century and it was actually kind of…depressing.

Grabbing her purse, she was about to walk out the door when she had an idea. She knew she may regret it, but Melanie also knew she wanted to do something to make Josiah smile, just like he had done for her so many times since they'd met.

Feeling a little more excited than she thought she would, Melanie walked outside and walked right up to Josiah and kissed him soundly on the lips.

"You all right?" he asked.

Taking his hands in hers, she pulled him close. "It occurred to me when I went to get my purse that there is a lot of open space in the cabin."

Josiah looked over her shoulder toward the house and then back to her. "You want to go to the mall and get some furniture?"

She laughed. "No, I don't want to go to the mall," she sighed dramatically. "I was thinking maybe you might want to…set up your tree and your Christmas decorations in the cabin."

His eyes went wide and then he smiled bigger and brighter than she'd ever seen. "Really? You mean it?"

She nodded and then let out a little scream when he lifted her up and spun her around before kissing her.

Yeah, this was definitely the right decision.

Chapter Six

Josiah had thought Melanie would put up more of a resistance regarding the decorations. Hell, he even thought he was going to have to come right out and ask her if he could do it—he never thought she would have offered so quickly.

Yeah, she was softening toward the whole Christmas thing and the thought made him smile.

Once the decision was made, they went to the diner for some lunch and then to Josiah's storage unit to get his Christmas decorations. They brought everything back to the cabin and stacked all of the boxes in the living room. Melanie didn't ask what was in any of them or why there were so many; she simply worked alongside of him.

When everything was stacked up, she turned to him with a big smile on her face. "Now what?"

Josiah looked around the room and already knew how he wanted to decorate it, but they were missing one key thing. "Now we go and chop down a tree."

Melanie's eyes went wide. "Chop one down? Don't…don't you have…like, you know…an artificial one?"

He made a tsk-ing sound. "Never in my entire life have we had a fake tree. We always went and cut one down." Taking her by the hand, he gently tugged her behind him as he went back outside.

"Now? We're going to go and do this now?" she cried.

Josiah nodded. "If it's all right with you, I think we can find a great one right here on the property. Carol used to plant them as seedlings years ago. I think we'll be able to find a good one." He looked at her and smiled. "You up for the hunt?"

Melanie looked around. "How big is this property again?"

"About fifteen acres."

She groaned. "Maybe…maybe you should go alone and do it. It will be faster that way. I'll stay here and make some cocoa."

His eyes lit up. "I have an even better idea," he began. "I have a thermos at my place. Why don't you make the cocoa while I go and grab the thermos and some supplies and we'll head out together?"

"Josiah…"

"It'll be fun," he said. "I promise." He gave her his most charming smile in hopes of winning her over. She looked at him and he could see the reluctance in her eyes and knew he had to be careful not to push too hard or all of this could just blow up in his face. "Please," he added softly.

Melanie's shoulders sagged as she nodded. "Okay. Let me get started on the cocoa."

Josiah reached for her and pulled her into his arms and kissed her on the tip of her nose. "Thank you."

She looked up at him curiously. "For what?"

"The last few years, I've gone out and done this myself. Before that I had my dad with me or at least one sibling. It's nice to have someone with me for company and I'm really glad it's you."

Everything about her seemed to soften at his words. "I'm not swinging the axe though," she warned. "I'll be more than happy to stand back and watch, but I'm definitely not cutting anything."

"That's fine," he smiled. "I'll be back in a few minutes." He watched Melanie walk back into the cabin before going over to his own place and getting the needed supplies.

With his backpack filled with everything they needed, Josiah walked back over to the cabin and let himself in.

"Just in time," Melanie said from the kitchen. "Cocoa is ready. Do you have the thermos?"

He held up a large silver thermos.

"Good grief," she chuckled. "How many cups is that thing?"

"It holds six cups," he said nonchalantly. "Why?"

"How long do you plan on us being out there?"

"I don't think we'll need to drink all six cups but it's the only one I have so…" he shrugged. Noticing she was still a bit wide-eyed, Josiah walked over to her and poured the cocoa into the thermos himself and then put the lid on. "Ready?"

"I just need to grab my hat and gloves," she said as she walked to the front closet to get them. "How long does it normally take you to find a good tree?"

"It varies. I mean, some years I've walked into the woods and spotted it right away. Other years it's taken a couple of hours."

"Oh."

"Come on, Mel," he said, taking her hands in his. "Don't be like that. You're looking for it to be over before it's even begun."

Her shoulders sagged. "It's just…you know how I feel about all of this," she began diplomatically. "I'm willing to have the decorations and all, but…I just don't see why we need to walk around in the freezing cold to find a tree. There are dozens of Christmas tree lots all over town. Why can't we just go to one of them? It would be faster, we wouldn't have to lug a tree all over the property and we can be back here snuggled in front of the fire much sooner." She batted her lashes at him.

"So you're saying if I opt to get a pre-cut tree— and totally break Stone family tradition—you'll have a better attitude about the entire process?"

Melanie nodded. "Work with me, Josiah," she said sweetly. "I'm already in this for decorations and a damn parade. Don't get greedy."

Her words could have been firm, but her lips were tilted in a sassy smirk and Josiah knew when to quit pushing his luck. He hated the thought of not cutting down his own tree, but if it meant Melanie wouldn't be quite so hostile about it, then maybe it was a fair compromise. After all, maybe next year he could ease her into going out into the woods to cut down their tree.

Whoa…wait a minute. He needed to stop that right now. It was hard enough just getting her through this Christmas. There was no guarantee what was going to happen next year.

But a man could hope.

"Okay, fine," he said casually. "We'll hit the tree lots and see what we can find."

"Good."

"But," he added quickly, "I want you to actively help me choose."

"What? Why?" she asked nervously, nibbling her bottom lip.

Josiah stepped in close. "Because I didn't suggest us doing this so it could be torture for you. It's something fun for us to do together. We'll find a tree and come back here and trim it and decorate it." He grinned. "And it's much better when you go into it with a good attitude and not snarl at the tree."

"I haven't snarled at anything," she grumbled. "Yet."

"My point exactly." He kissed the top of her head. "If I can't go hunting to cut down my own tree, you can't snarl. Deal?"

She eyed him suspiciously, but agreed. "Deal."

****

City sidewalks, busy sidewalks, dressed in holiday style…

If it wasn't for the blaring sounds of "Silver Bells" playing in the Christmas tree lot, Melanie would have to admit she was having a good time. She and Josiah were slowly walking up and down the rows of trees critiquing each one—too tall, too skinny, too fat, bald spots—she had no idea there was so much consideration that went into finding a Christmas tree. Back when they did celebrate, Melanie and her father had an artificial tree they put out every year. This live tree thing was a completely new experience.

"Okay," Josiah said, interrupting her thoughts. "What do you think?"

In the air there's a feeling of Christmas.

Melanie slowly walked around the tree, as Josiah taught her to do. She inspected it from every angle—touching it, searching for any gaps and bald spots—before answering. "I think it could be a contender. No obvious gaps. It has a good size and color." She looked at him hopefully. "What do you think?"

Children laughing, people passing…

"I do like it…"

'But…"

"But," he said, "I just don't…love it."

Melanie rolled her eyes. It wasn't the first time he'd said that phrase. Seriously? He had to *love* the tree? What in the world?

"I can hear you mocking me from here," he said.

"I didn't say a word!" she laughed.

"You didn't have to. Your face said it all." Josiah placed the tree back in its spot and faced her. "Well?"

She sighed. "Okay, fine. I don't understand what all the fuss is! It's a perfectly good tree! It's the fourth perfectly good tree we've found. I just don't get what the big deal is!"

Afraid she had hurt his feelings or perhaps made him angry, she was surprised when he gave her a lopsided grin. "You'll understand when we get it home and decorate it. Trust me. When it's the perfect tree—one that you love—it makes all the difference." Looking over his shoulder, Josiah glanced around the tree lot. "Maybe we need to go to another lot. I'm just not feeling it at this one."

"Are you sure? Or are you just not feeling it because it's a lot and not the woods?"

He looked at her, his smile dropping slightly. "I'm not going to lie to you, Melanie, this is the first time in my entire life I'm doing this so you have to give me a break."

"It's my first time too," she countered, "and you're not giving me much of a break."

They were at a bit of a standoff and she wasn't sure who was going to cave first.

Ring-a-ling…hear them ring…soon it will be Christmas day.

Josiah seemed to relax a bit and he sighed. "You're right. I'm being a bit overly critical about the entire thing. Although I do have to say that I'm just not impressed with this lot. Do you mind if we go to another one?"

Knowing this was a big deal for him, she agreed. Together they walked back to his car and made their way to the next tree lot which was just two blocks away. As soon as Melanie stepped out of the car, she groaned.

Silver Bells…Silver Bells…It's Christmas time in the city…

"You okay?" Josiah asked as he walked around the car to her.

"This song is…" she stopped and took a deep breath, then let it out. "It's just everywhere."

He chuckled and took one of her hands in his and led her toward the rows of trees. "It's the town's claim to fame. You get used to it."

For a minute she wanted to argue and say it would never happen, but she didn't want to ruin the moment.

They walked up and down the first two rows without much luck when suddenly she saw it.

The tree.

For the life of her, Melanie didn't know how she knew, but she just did. Josiah was busy looking at one tree and she walked ahead of him to "the one." Without alerting him, she did all the things he had done with the previous trees.

This is Santa's big scene…

She moved it out and away from the other trees and then inspected it. Touching the branches, she inhaled the scent of pine and smiled. It was a good height, a good width and from what she was able to see, there were no visible gaps. "How about this one?" she called out to him without really looking in his direction. It wasn't until she turned and looked at him that she saw he was only a few feet away and smiling at her. "What? What's the matter?"

Rather than answer, Josiah walked around the tree making his own observations. Melanie kept waiting for him to say whether he liked it or not—although she couldn't imagine him *not* liking it because it was perfect. When he stood next to her and crossed his arms over his chest and frowned, she wanted to stamp her foot in frustration.

"Well?" she finally asked. "If I'm not allowed to frown at the trees, neither are you."

"I'm not frowning," he said quietly.

"It sure looks like a frown. Or maybe a pout. What's wrong? I thought I did a good job," she said and suddenly felt a little self-conscious about the whole thing.

After what seemed like an eternity, Josiah turned to her with a slow grin. "You actually did a great job. I love it. This is the one."

She almost sagged to the ground with relief. "Really?"

He nodded. "Yeah, really." Taking the tree from her hands, he motioned for one of the employees to come and get it for them.

"So if you liked it, why were you frowning?"

Josiah waited until the employee had taken the tree from them before turning and wrapping Melanie in his arms. "I guess I've gotten used to being the one to find the perfect tree. And you went and found it first."

Unable to help herself, she laughed out loud. "I can't believe we're having this conversation over a tree!"

"Not just any tree—a Christmas tree!" he countered.

"Still a tree," she said. "But I'm glad you approved. I was walking toward it and…I just knew."

His smile turned knowing.

"What? What's that look about?"

"I'm just happy that we found a tree."

Melanie snuggled closer to him. "Me too."

Pulling back, Josiah looked down at her. 'Really?"

She nodded. "It's freezing out here. I'm ready to go home."

It wasn't the only reason she was glad they had found a tree, but she couldn't quite figure out why. The whole experience had been more fun than she would have imagined and the smell of pine was actually quite nice. And the thought of taking the tree home and decorating it with Josiah had her feeling a little bit giddy.

Maybe she'd bake a batch of sugar cookies for them for dessert…

Together they walked toward the exit to pay for the tree and get it tied to the car as the first snowflakes started to fall.

Soon it will be Christmas Day.

****

With a fire roaring in the fireplace and Melanie naked and wrapped in his arms on the living room floor in front of the newly-decorated Christmas tree, Josiah felt like life was just about perfect. He placed a kiss on the top of her head and gave a contented sigh.

"It's so pretty, don't you think?" she asked softly.

He nodded. "I certainly do. You picked a stellar tree."

She chuckled and reached for the blanket that had fallen behind them.

"Cold?"

"A little," she said. "Although with the fire in front of me and you behind me I shouldn't be."

Josiah helped her drape the blanket over them. "So you really like it? The tree?"

She nodded. "I really do. It's just so…sparkly." He could actually feel her smile even though she wasn't facing him. "And it smells so wonderful in here." Rolling over, she looked at him. "There were a lot of decorations in those boxes. Are they all yours or were some of them from your family?"

"My mom gave each of us kids a box of ornaments when we moved out—some were brand new but some were ones she knew were personal favorites from our childhood. Every year I add to the collection."

Melanie looked over her shoulder toward the tree. "Which ones did you add this year?"

"I haven't yet," he said softly, cupping her chin and gently forcing her to look at him. "It would mean a lot to me if you would pick one out for me."

Her blue eyes went wide. "Me?"

He nodded.

"But…but…"

"Melanie," he began, tilting his head forward so their heads were touching, "There are so many ornaments on the tree that have sentimental value to me; they remind me of things that are important. Things that I…love."

Josiah knew the moment he said it that Melanie knew what he meant because she gasped softly in his arms. Rather than saying it again and hearing her possibly come up with reasons why he couldn't feel the way he did or why she didn't return those feelings, he captured her lips and kissed her softly. He poured everything he felt but was suddenly too afraid to say into it, and when she wrapped her arms around him and pulled him close, he felt both lost and found at the same time.

****

Melanie stood with her back against the brick exterior wall of the chamber of commerce building and let out a breath. It was thirty degrees outside and all she wanted was a hot cup of cocoa and to be back at the cabin, curled up on the couch with a blanket and a good book.

And what was left of the sugar cookies.

Unfortunately, none of that wasn't on today's agenda.

All around her people were scurrying around with excitement. The annual Silver Bell Christmas Parade was due to start in less than an hour and she had gone over the schedule of events and had even smiled and done her best to show a little enthusiasm, but now that it was edging closer to go-time, nerves were kicking in.

A parade. Seriously, this is what her life had come to. When she had spoken to her father the night before and told him what she was doing, he was over the moon with excitement. For a minute she wondered if she had the wrong number because for as long as she could remember, her dad felt the same way she did about the holidays. Why was he now—all of a sudden—feeling festive? Which is what she asked him and he told her how going back to Silver Bell for just those two days had reminded him of how much he used to love Christmas.

Damn town.

Damn town and its stupid…

City sidewalks, busy sidewalks, dressed in holiday style…

"You have got to be kidding me!" she cried out and was instantly embarrassed when several people stopped and stared at her. Without saying a word, Melanie turned and walked around to the back of the building, away from prying eyes. It was like the damn song was mocking her. There were thousands of Christmas songs out there, so why couldn't they play another one? Where were Alvin and the Chipmunks when you really needed them?

Children laughing, People passing, Meeting smile after smile…

Taking a few steadying breaths, she did her best to calm down. It was just a song and it was just a parade—a ride in a car, really. So what was the big deal?

And on every street corner you'll hear…Silver Bells…Silver Bells…

Looking around, Melanie had to wonder how hard it would be to dismantle the town's sound system.

"There you are."

Melanie turned and saw Josiah walking toward her with his slow and easy gait and a smile on his handsome face. Just one look at him and she felt some of the tension easing from her body.

"You hiding out back here?"

"I needed a minute," she admitted.

"It's a lot of activity, I know. But in a few minutes, you'll be in the back of a really sporty convertible with a heated blanket and a cup of cocoa."

That made her feel a little bit better. Fishing into her coat pocket, she pulled out her iPod and showed it to him. "And I can block out some of the holiday music."

He shook his head and chuckled. "It's not so bad."

Reaching out, she clutched the front of his coat and shook him. "I would gladly get up and sing 'Jingle Bells' or 'Rudolph the Red Nosed Reindeer' if I never had to hear 'Silver Bells' again! Seriously, it's killing me!"

Rather than telling her she was crazy, Josiah hugged her close and then took the earbuds from her fingers and draped the cord around her and camouflaged it within her scarf so no one would see it. "What's on the playlist?" he asked.

"A little classic Motown, a little eighties rock…all of my faves."

He smiled at her and led her back toward all the activity. "So you'll get through the parade and at the end of the route, Erika Jacobs will meet you and bring you to the party tent where they have a table set up with a bunch of your books to sign."

Melanie nodded. "Got it."

"Then I'll meet you down there and we'll grab some lunch with everyone—they're serving a full-on turkey dinner with all the fixings."

"Sounds good."

"And afterwards, we're going to walk around and check out all the craft tables and I want you to pick out an ornament for the tree."

Looking up at him, she smiled. "Are you sure?"

"Have I lied about anything yet?"

She couldn't help but smile. "No."

"Then why would I start now? I want you to pick something for the tree. You've been good enough to let me put my tree up in your house and I think it would be nice for you to have something on there that you picked out."

Melanie didn't want to argue with him about it. She hadn't told him how much she was enjoying having the tree in the cabin or how much it meant to her that he wanted her to pick out ornaments for it. To be honest, she hadn't said a whole lot of anything since the day they'd put the tree up.

After Josiah's roundabout admission of love, Melanie had been a little shell-shocked. He might not have said it again, but the way he had made love to her afterwards spoke volumes. In the days that followed, he had worked extra hours and she had buckled down and was on a hot-streak with her writing. The only time they seemed to see one another was late at night before they went to bed, and when Josiah got up to leave for work in the morning. It wasn't an ideal schedule, but for each of them, their jobs were top priority.

Today was the first time they were spending quality time together in more than a week.

She just wished it were someplace other than a damn Christmas parade.

He must have sensed the direction of her thoughts because he stopped walking and turned her to face him. "It's a parade, not an execution. If you just pretend it's a parade for something else, will that put a smile on your face?"

With a small shrug she looked up at him. "Kind of hard to pretend it's not a Christmas parade when I have dancing reindeer circling the car."

"Mel, please try to relax. After we finish up here, how about we go home, get dressed up and go someplace nice for dinner?"

It was on the tip of her tongue to say something about them finding a place to go that didn't play Christmas music, but she knew she would be asking for the impossible. "That sounds wonderful." For a moment she paused. "Then I have one request for after dinner."

Josiah's eyes widened for a brief moment before he broke out in a sexy grin. "Oh yeah?"

Playfully smacking his arm she said, "I'm serious."

He tried to look properly chastised but it just made Melanie giggle.

"After dinner, I'd like us to spend the night at your place."

Brows furrowed, he looked at her as if she were crazy. "My place? The tiny house?"

Melanie nodded.

"Why?"

"We're always in the cabin…"

"Because it's bigger."

She smiled patiently at him. "Yes, it's bigger, but I'd like to spend some time in your space. And besides, I think I'd really like to sleep up in the loft. I bet on a starry night it's magnificent to see out the skylight."

Nodding in agreement, Josiah looked about ready to say something when Erika Jacobs—who owned the local bookstore—walked over and interrupted them. She was decked out in red and white with a big furry hat and Melanie thought she looked a lot like Mrs. Claus.

"Hey, Sheriff," she said with a smile and then turned to Melanie with an even bigger smile. "Hey, Melanie. You all ready? The car and blanket are all ready for you!"

Melanie stifled a groan and reluctantly stepped away from Josiah. He gave her a thumbs up and watched her walk away.

"I want you to know that your publisher has been a dream to work with," Erika said. "They sent over about a dozen copies of all eight of your books and people are so excited to meet you! I think you're going to run out of books super quickly. I brought over the inventory I had in my store too just in case we need them."

Forcing a smile, Melanie thanked her and was grateful people were quickly being herded to their positions and told to be ready.

"I'll be waiting for you at the end of the parade route to take you to the tent," Erika said as she adjusted the blanket over Melanie's lap and handed her the large insulated cup of hot chocolate. "Smile and wave and have fun!" she called out before bustling away.

Driving the car was Ed Kincaid. He was in his seventies and had an easy smile –, which Melanie only caught a quick glance of because the scarf he immediately wrapped around his neck went all the way up and over his nose.

With a sigh, Melanie made herself comfortable, got her iPod ready and put her earbuds in and pulled her hat down over her ears for a little more warmth.

Within minutes, they started moving. It was at a snail's pace, but they were moving. For a minute, Melanie could only stare. There were hundreds of people lining the streets—hundreds! For such a small town, it seemed like this parade drew people in from miles around!

It wasn't a hardship to smile and wave and, since she had gotten distracted and hadn't turned on her music, she was surprised to hear people calling out her name and how they loved her books!

The kids who were dancing around her car were very talented and the marching band ahead of them was actually quite good! Before she knew it, they were coming around the last bend in the route and there was a crew of people waving Ed on to the parking area. And there was Erika - with a big smile on her face, waiting to help Melanie from the car.

Before she could climb out, a trio of dancers came over to her and asked for her autograph. The girls were all high-school students and Melanie loved that they knew who she was. Reading their names that were on the back of their costumes—Kori, Leah and Cherie—she thanked them and signed the papers they had scrounged up for her.

Stepping down, she thanked Ed before turning her attention to Erika. "That seemed fast!"

Erika's smile deepened. "That was almost forty minutes from start to finish for you! If it felt quick, it just means you were having a good time!"

There was no way she was admitting to that, but she returned Erika's smile and followed her into a large party tent. As soon as she stepped inside,

Melanie was surprised by the warmth. "Are there heaters in here?" she asked.

"Only a few, but it really does make a difference. The sheriff asked if we could place your table near one of them since you're not used to the cold temperatures." They stopped in front of a long table that was brightly decorated with banners with Melanie's picture and book covers on it.

"Oh my goodness," she said. "Did my publisher send the banner?"

Erika blushed. "I actually had it made. I know everything was such short notice and I have a little bit of a gift for graphic design and the internet made it easy to order."

"It's wonderful!" Melanie said, and she meant it. She had banners for events before but never one that was so eye catching. "I love it!"

"Really?" Erika asked, her face glowing.

Melanie nodded. "Definitely! I may ask you to design all of my banners from now on!"

For a minute she thought the older woman was going to cry but instead she grabbed Melanie and hugged her tight. "You have no idea how much that means to me." She stepped away and wiped at her eyes. "My ex-husband always told me I wasn't talented and had no skills. So to hear someone like you praise my work just means the world to me."

Melanie made a mental note to reach out to Erika again for banners and maybe more graphics for future books. "Should I take a seat?" she asked.

For the next few minutes, Erika helped her get settled and showed her where her extra pens were along with extra books. "We have an assistant for you too," Erika explained. "Aimee's a senior at Silver Bell Falls High School and she's interested in journalism. She was very excited when we told her she'd be assisting you."

Melanie took her seat and smiled. "Well then, I can't wait to meet her."

"And if either of you need anything and can't find me, just ask for Ruth, Shelly, Sue or Chrissy—Aimee knows who they are—and they'll get it for you. They're all part of the committee."

For the next two hours, Melanie signed books. She ran out of them and then was signing pretty much anything people could find for her to sign. Aimee was by her side and would get up and get her something to drink or snack on and even managed to scrounge up some flyers that Erika quickly threw together with Melanie's book covers on them.

By the time Josiah came for her, she was completely exhausted. "So you sold out of all of them, huh?" he asked, grinning from ear to ear.

It was the first time that had happened for her at an event and Melanie had to admit it felt pretty darn good. "I couldn't believe how quickly they went," she said as she stood up. After introducing Josiah to Aimee, Melanie thanked the girl for all of her help and promised to look over a short story she'd written for one of her classes. Taking Josiah's hand, she made her way around the table and they began walking around the room to see the rest of the craft vendors.

"So…" he began, "did you have a good time?"

"You know what? I did," she said, looking up at him with a big smile on her face. They walked hand in hand through the crowd, talking to people as they made their way around and looked at the different holiday crafts that people were selling. "The fans were amazing and I couldn't believe how many of them there were! They were even calling out to me on the parade route!"

"Some of them had signs too," Josiah said playfully as he nudged her shoulder. "I think there was a trio of ladies near the end of the route who even had a banner with your picture on it!"

"I know! That was…" She paused and thought about it for a minute, "Alima, Isha and Michele! They were so friendly and super sweet and I think I'm going to their book club meeting next week. Honestly, Josiah, this was probably the most enthusiastic crowd I've ever had at a signing. They were wonderful."

"I knew they would be."

Melanie had no idea what it was she was looking for as they strolled around but she was simply having a good time looking. There were tables loaded with everything from cakes and cookies to holiday home décor like candles and centerpieces. She and Josiah stopped and talked to a ton of different people and as they came around to the last row of tables, she saw someone who seemed to be selling ornaments. "Oooh!" she cried. "Look! We need to go over there!" Tugging Josiah with her, they made their way over to the table.

For several minutes she looked at the variety of handmade ornaments. Some were ceramic, some were blown glass and some were made of wood. Melanie picked up one and then another and then another until she found it.

The perfect ornament.

It was a small wooden wreath with a heart in the middle that simply said "love." It was hand-painted and everything about it seemed to speak to Melanie. Within minutes, she had paid for it and had it wrapped in tissue paper in a small gift bag. When she turned to Josiah, he had that look on his face—the same one he had the day they'd made love in front of their tree.

"It seemed like the perfect ornament," she said quietly.

He swallowed hard and if she didn't know any better, she'd say he was too choked up to speak. All he did was nod and pull her in close to kiss her on the top of her head.

They casually made their way out of the tent and to Josiah's car. He held the door open for her and before she climbed in, she stopped and studied him. "You okay?"

He nodded again.

"Did you like the ornament I picked?"

Another nod.

"Oh." A little part of her was disappointed. It wasn't as if she wanted him to throw a parade in her honor over an ornament, but it would have been nice if he at least told her—with words—that he liked it. She was just about to sit down when Josiah's hand on her arm stopped her. She looked up at him expectantly.

"Every year I come to this craft fair," he began quietly. "I have to be here in official capacity but I always take time to walk around and check out everyone's tables and compliment them on what they've made." He paused. "For the last several years, whenever I stop at Hank and Lisa's table, I think about how incredible their ornaments are."

"Hank and Lisa?"

"They're the ones who made your ornament," he clarified. "Hank does all the woodwork by hand. He's been doing it for years and I've always marveled at it but never bought anything. And then today, you saw them and it was like…you knew."

This time it was Melanie's turn to nod because that's exactly what it was like. And there was nothing she could say, because without any words, they managed to say it all.

Chapter Seven

A week before Christmas, Josiah walked into Melanie's bedroom and froze. "You're packing?"

Looking over her shoulder at him, she nodded.

"But…why? You still have another six weeks here. And…and Christmas is a week away. We said we'd spend it together." Everything in him was in panic mode and he didn't know how to stop it.

"I sent my rough draft of the book to my editor on Monday. She'd been so anxious about it that I sent it without doing any of my own edits," Melanie said while still folding clothes. "Anyway, she got it and she loves it. I need to go into Manhattan for a few days to meet with her and while I'm there I'm also meeting with my grandmother's attorney."

Josiah frowned. "For what?"

"I never contacted him like I said I would about starting the paperwork for me so I could sell the property to you at the end of the three months."

It wasn't supposed to happen like this, he thought. She wasn't supposed to still be thinking about selling him the property or leaving because in his mind, she was always going to stay. Walking over to her, he gently grasped her shoulders and turned her to face him. "Mel, I don't understand what's going on."

She looked at him curiously. "It's pretty obvious, Josiah. I need to go away for a few days and take care of some things. I'm coming back."

He wanted to relax—maybe even sigh with relief—but he felt like her leaving was going to change everything. "You're sure you're coming back?" he asked tentatively.

Melanie smiled at him. "Of course I'm coming back. I have six more weeks that I have to stay here for."

Josiah's hands instantly dropped away and he took a few steps back and cursed.

"What? What's the matter?"

This wasn't the discussion he wanted to have and he hated feeling like he was forced into it, but clearly there were some things that needed to be said. "Is that the only reason you're coming back? Because your grandmother's will dictates it?"

The smile she gave him was patient and it just irritated him even more.

"I'm serious, Melanie," he snapped. "We've spent every day together for six weeks! I thought we were building something here but at the end of the day, you're still going around treating this like it's some sort of arrangement!"

"That's not true!" she cried.

"Then tell me how it is that with everything we've shared you can still stand here and talk about leaving at the end of January! How is it that you're still focused on selling me this property?"

"You want this property! Hell, you should have gotten it, not me! We both know that! I'm just trying to make it right!"

He raked a hand through his hair in frustration. He cursed again. "I don't give a damn about the property! It's you that I want!"

Her shoulders sagged and she slowly approached him. "I want you too, Josiah. I just don't want this hanging between us. I know what it's like to want something so badly and then have it taken away. I've lived with it my whole life. You gave up so much in hopes of buying this land. I just want to get through the three months so we can do it right and then I can sign it over to you and it will be yours and everything will be okay."

"Wait, wait, wait...sign it over to me?" he asked incredulously. "What does that mean?"

She sighed. "I wanted it to be a surprise. I'm not selling the property to you; I'm going to the lawyer so I can simply sign it over to you when the terms of the will are met. Then it will be yours."

He shook his head. "Uh-uh. No way. You're not signing anything over to me. I am buying the property from you at market value. That's not negotiable."

"Why are you being so stubborn about this?" she cried with frustration.

"Because it's not right! I've planned on buying this land for years! I've worked my ass off to save the money for it and there's no way I'm going to just take it. I'm not a charity case!"

"Josiah," she began, trying to sound calmer, "it's not charity. This should have been yours to begin with. I have no ties to this place—you do. Please. I want this to be yours."

Her words should have made him feel better, but they didn't. "The property could be ours, Mel," he said. "Yours and mine. I love you. I want to marry you. There's no reason to draw up contracts or talk to lawyers. I want us to be together and we can start a life together here. We can tear down the cabin and build a place that is well and truly ours." His heart was beating like he'd run a marathon and it wasn't until he was done speaking that he saw Melanie had paled and she wasn't smiling.

Maybe he was speaking too soon or maybe he shouldn't have blurted it out quite like he did but…he had seriously hoped for a different reaction. "I've never hidden how I feel about you," he said gruffly. "I know in the beginning we said this was a temporary thing but somewhere along the way, that changed." He paused and saw her expression hadn't changed. "I guess it was only for me."

Melanie let out a shaky breath. "You have to know how much you mean to me," she said quietly. "I never expected this—you—any of it. I was so angry when I got here and then there you were and you…you make me see things differently. I'm not so angry anymore and for that I will always be thankful."

Josiah wasn't sure what she was getting at but so far it wasn't a declaration of love.

"Melanie, I love you. I fell in love with you when you were angry and when you resented the fact that you had to be here. I love our talks and the way you're so open about your feelings." He paused again. "But I need to know how you feel about me. Call it insecurity or at this point just damn curiosity, but I need to know where I stand with you."

Her blue eyes welled with tears. "You mean the world to me," she said quietly. "When you're not here, I miss you so much that it scares me."

He hated how needy he sounded. "But…"

"But we haven't talked about so many things. In your mind you see us married and living here in

Silver Bell and building a house and a life here. That's your dream but…I'm not so sure it's mine."

Okay. Wow. Josiah had no idea what to do with that. "Is it me or is it the town?"

She visibly swallowed. "I have a life back in Raleigh. My father is there. My friends are there. My house is there. Josiah, I…I just don't know if I can walk away from all of it."

He took a step away from her and then another. "But you can walk away from me."

"Don't…" she said, reaching for him but her feet never moved. "It's not like that."

He smiled at her sadly. "It's exactly like that," he said and then turned and walked out of the room. Out of the house.

And quite possibly, out of her life.

****

She stood there long after the front door had closed. So many feelings were running through her— anxiety, fear, sadness, anger—and she wasn't sure which one was at the top of the list. Her heart beat madly as she slowly left the room and walked out to the living room. The Christmas scene there seemed to mock her.

Another Christmas ruined.

Perfect.

The night before, Josiah had put what seemed like a small mountain of gifts under the tree. He had said they were gifts for his family but there were no tags on any of them and she had a sneaky suspicion they were for her. Ironically, she had a pile of gifts for him hidden away in her bedroom closet. As much as it pained her to admit it, she had really been looking forward to Christmas this year. For the first time in…forever…she had been hopeful. But the universe won out because it clearly wanted her never to enjoy a Christmas again.

Ever.

****

All Josiah wanted to do was pace, but it wasn't nearly as satisfying when he was doing it in such a confined space. The whole damn tiny house thing had seemed so perfect and logical at one point, but right now it just pissed him off.

And to be honest, he wasn't sure which particular topic pissed him off more—the fact that Melanie was going out of town without talking to him about it, that she still planned on going back to Raleigh at the end of three months and just walking away from their relationship, or maybe the fact that she had planned on giving him the damn property as if he were a charity case.

Or maybe, just maybe, it was that even though he said the words to her out loud and told her he loved her, she still hadn't said it back.

Right now, all of it was fighting for the top spot and there wasn't a damn thing he could do about it. She had to go and meet with her publisher—that was a given. It was her job, her livelihood and there was no way he would tell her or ask her not to go. But the lawyer? Yeah, that was a completely different story.

They hadn't talked about it—not since those first few days and to be honest, Josiah had forgotten about it. That probably had something to do with him not wanting to think about the end of the three months Melanie was supposed to be there. Call it delusional, but in his mind, she wasn't going to go back to Raleigh. Well, that wasn't completely true. He knew she was going to have to go back there to tie up loose ends, but in the end she was going to be with him in Silver Bell.

Clearly he was wrong.

Yeah, yeah, yeah…she said she was coming back after her meetings and how she'd stay the three months and how he meant the world to her.

The world.

Not love.

Dammit.

So now what? She was going to be gone for a few days and Christmas was right around the corner. Her gifts were under the tree and he had planned on sweeping her off her feet. How could he possibly go through with it now? If they weren't heading in the same direction, how was he supposed to sit there and spend Christmas with her without slowly devastating himself?

It sucked. The entire situation sucked.

The silver lining—if he had to find one—was that he was apparently going to have a few days to think about it and figure out what it was he was supposed to do. Did he continue to woo her when she came back or give her space?

"I have no freaking idea," he muttered and sat down on his sofa, closing his eyes as he threw his head back. "No freaking clue at all."

It was dark out and if he knew one thing, it was that Melanie wasn't leaving tonight. She wasn't going to fly out or drive six hours to get to Manhattan until tomorrow at least.

He'd offer to go with her, but it wouldn't solve anything. The time apart would be helpful for him to get his head together and figure out what he was going to do. And maybe it would help Melanie by giving her time to think about Josiah's proposal for their future.

****

The following evening, Melanie sat in her upscale hotel room in Manhattan staring out at the skyline and sighed. Josiah hadn't come back to the cabin and she took a cab to the airport. She hated leaving things the way they had, but there hadn't been much of a choice.

All day he had been on her mind—to the point that her editor playfully smacked her in the head and told her to snap out of it. It was exactly what she needed and from that point on, even though he was still there, Melanie was able to engage in her meeting about the Christmas book. Her entire editing team was thrilled with what she'd written and they brainstormed together and worked through the weak points. When someone asked her what had finally inspired her, Josiah's name was the first thing that came to mind.

After the meeting, Christine had taken her to dinner and questioned her a lot more about what had finally gotten her out of her funk. That's when Melanie pretty much broke down and shared the whole story of her relationship with Josiah. It felt so good to talk to someone about it and she was thankful Liza simply let her talk before offering any suggestions.

"It seems to me you're in love with him," Christine said. "It's obvious. So why are you fighting it?"

"I'm not fighting it. Not really," Melanie replied weakly.

"So what's the hang-up?"

Melanie looked at her and felt like she was on the verge of tears. "It's so soon," she cried. "And we don't agree on where it is we see ourselves living."

"It's because it's a Christmas town, isn't it?"

Melanie nodded.

Elbows on the table, Christine leaned toward her. "Okay, at the end of the day, what matters more to you—being with Josiah or not dealing with the biggest holiday of the year?"

"That's not fair, Chris! It's not that simple!"

"So make it that simple! What's so great about living in Raleigh? You're a writer and you can work from anywhere!"

"My father is in Raleigh—and my house, my friends…everything!"

"Have you talked to your father about it?"

Melanie hesitated.

"That's what I thought," Christine said confidently, leaning back in her chair. "Look, I can sit here all night and tell you why you should do it, but it's something only you can decide. I know you and your dad are super close so really, you need to talk to him. Maybe he can give you some direction."

Now, hours later, Melanie knew she needed to take that advice. Grabbing her phone, she sat on the bed and called her father.

"Hey! There's my girl!" he said, just like he always did. "Are you going to have a white Christmas in Silver Bell this year?"

Just the mention of the town made Melanie's stomach clench. "I don't know," she said with a small chuckle. "I haven't really been watching the weather."

"Why not? There is nothing better than snow for Christmas. It just makes everything more magical."

Ugh. Now her father was sounding like one of Santa's elves. Yikes. "Are you busy right now?" she asked nervously. "Do you have time to talk?"

John paused for a minute. "Of course, sweetheart. What's going on?"

For the next few minutes, she shared what had been going on between her and Josiah and the argument they'd had. "So?" she asked. "What did I do that was so wrong?"

"Oh, Mel," John began, "Sweetheart, I had no idea you had this many issues."

"Wait…what? What exactly does that mean?"

"It means I never should have let my disillusionment rub off on you. I didn't realize how down you had gotten on Christmas."

"Okay, can we just move past Christmas for a minute?" she huffed. "I don't understand why he's so upset! He knows I have a life back in Raleigh. This isn't new information! Why is he suddenly making a big deal out of it?"

"Mel, he's in love with you. He told you that. Of course he's going to make a big deal out of you wanting to leave him when your three months is up. He's thinking about and planning a future with you and you're thinking about and planning on leaving him. How could he not be upset?"

She sighed. "I…I didn't quite see it that way."

"How did you see it?"

"I thought," she shrugged, "I thought we'd get through the three months, I'd give him the property and come home. Then we'd do the long-distance thing until we knew each other better then…take it from there."

"I see two things wrong with your plan," John stated.

"And they are?"

"For starters, you're giving him the property."

"What's wrong with that?" she cried. "Geez, I thought I was doing a good thing and everyone thinks it's so wrong!"

"You hurt his pride, Mel. You didn't talk to him about it. Men are funny in situations like this. He's been working so hard toward this goal and you just made it seem like it was all for nothing."

"That wasn't my intention…"

"No, but the result was the same."

She sighed. "Well damn. So what do I do?"

"We'll get to that in a minute," he said before clearing his throat. "Let's deal with the long-distance thing next."

"If we have to…"

"We do," he said firmly. "Let me ask you something, how much do you love your house here in Raleigh?"

Melanie thought about it for a minute. "I can't say that I love it. It needs a lot of work, it's not in my ideal neighborhood, but it was in my budget and it was an investment."

"Okay," he continued, "and how much time and money do you plan on putting into it to make it a place you love?"

She shrugged again. "I don't know. Not much. I had a five-year plan. I'd live there and then sell it. That's it. I never intended to do extensive renovations."

"And how often do you go out with your friends?"

That was a good question. It had been a while. "Maybe once a month?"

"So then let me ask you…what's holding you here? It seems to me like you're not particularly loving Raleigh."

"You're there," she said defensively. "Why would I want to move so far away from you? We're family! We've only got each other!"

John took a moment and Melanie heard his soft sigh. "You want to know the truth, Mel?"

"Of course I do."

"We stayed here because I didn't want to move you away from your friends when you were younger. Then you went to college here and then…there didn't seem to be a reason to move anymore."

"Wait, are you saying you wanted to move when I was younger?"

"Oh absolutely," John replied.

"To where?"

"Do you really want to know?"

"Dad, I wouldn't have asked if I didn't," Melanie said wearily.

"Silver Bell Falls."

For a minute, she thought she misunderstood him. "Excuse me?"

"You heard me. If I could have picked us up and moved anywhere, I would have chosen Silver Bell Falls. I spent a lot of time there when I was growing up and…I don't know…it was just the ideal place to me."

"Ugh…what is it with that town?" she sighed and flopped back on the hotel bed. "I just don't get it!"

"No, I think you do get it but you're fighting it. What I don't understand is why."

"You lost me, Dad."

"Have you made friends there?" John asked.

"Sure. Josiah has introduced me to just about everyone in the entire town. And then at the parade I feel like I met all of them again and their friends!"

"Were they nice?"

"What does…?"

"Just answer the question, Mel," he chuckled.

"Of course they were nice! I didn't realize people could seriously be that nice!"

"It's a pretty town," he went on. "Peaceful and there are some amazing places within a short driving distance. The weather isn't ideal but there's a lot to be said about winter activities. You never experienced anything like it so you don't understand, but it can be a lot of fun."

"Dad…"

"And what about Josiah? How do you feel about him?"

This was not the conversation she wanted to be having. Here she was thinking her dad would understand her—side with her—and it was starting to feel like he was just as against her as everyone else seemed to be.

"Come on, Mel. There's nothing you can't tell me." He paused. "Do you love him?"

"We've only known each other for six weeks. How can I possibly be in love? It's too soon. I don't know him well enough yet."

"Sweetheart, your mother and I dated all through high school—four years. And in the end, I still didn't know her. It's not about how long you know someone that equals whether or not you can be in love with them. Sometimes you just know." He waited a minute. "So I'll ask you again, do you love him?"

"I do," she said quietly. "I really do."

"So what are you waiting for? Don't fight this, Mel. You'll regret it. Believe me. Don't pass up the chance to find your happiness."

"Did you? Did you pass up your chance?" she asked, feeling like they were being honest for the first time.

"I fear I did," he admitted. "I spent so many years being devastated by your mom leaving us, that I missed out on making a better life for you and me. Maybe I would have met somebody new. Maybe if I had moved us someplace else, we both could have started over."

"It's never too late, Dad. You're not tied to Raleigh either. No one says you have to stay there."

"You're right," he said after a long moment. "If I'm going to sit here and preach to you, perhaps I should be taking my own advice."

Melanie couldn't help but smile. "Exactly. So what do we do now?"

"Well, I can't speak for you but I think I'm going to start putting out feelers to find a job and relocate."

Her smile grew. "Any place in particular you're thinking of?"

"I have a few places in mind," he said with a lightness that gave Melanie hope. "What about you? What are you going to do?"

"I have a meeting with the attorney tomorrow and one more meeting with Christine and my flight home is Thursday morning."

"Thursday? But you'll be done with your business tomorrow night? Why stay in the city for an extra day?"

"Because it's New York City, Dad! I don't get here very often and…now that I'm not quite so anti-Christmas, I'm actually enjoying all of the decorations and window displays."

"But Saturday is Christmas Eve. Isn't that cutting it a little close?"

"It is what it is and with the way Josiah and I left things, I'm not so sure I'm going to have anyone to be with on Christmas Eve."

"I'm sure you will. Couples fight all the time. It doesn't mean you have to break up or never speak to each other again."

"I hope you're right."

"On this one, I speak from experience."

****

Josiah stood in the baggage claim area and kept watching for Melanie. They still hadn't spoken since the night he'd walked out of the cabin, but when she texted him last night and asked if he would pick her up at the airport, he said yes.

The time alone had been a blessing. He had been able to sit and think with no distractions and he knew without a doubt, he would wait for her. If Melanie wanted to go back to Raleigh and do a long-distance relationship, he'd do it. He wouldn't like it, but he'd do it.

Because he loved her.

And seeing her some of the time was better than never seeing her again.

He was so lost in thought, he didn't notice her approach. He simply blinked and she was there. "Hey."

Melanie's smile was a little shy. "Hey."

It was so good to see her and he wanted to pick her up in his arms and kiss her, but he wasn't sure if that was what she wanted. So he decided to play it safe. "How was your flight?"

"Good," she replied. "Crowded, but good."

He nodded and knew he was smiling, but it felt a little forced. Together they waited for her one piece of luggage and then walked out to his car. Out of the corner of his eye, he saw Melanie shiver multiple times and it only stood to remind him how she wasn't used to the winters here—the temperatures in Raleigh were milder.

Once they were on the road, he asked her how her meetings went with her publisher and editor and that managed to fill the bulk of the hour-long drive back to the cabin. She was very animated when she spoke about her work and Josiah knew this book in particular had been a major achievement for her on many levels. He was proud of her.

"I know it's a little late, but did you have dinner before you took off?" he asked.

Melanie shook her head. "I had a late lunch and thought maybe we'd stop at the grocery store on the way home and grab something."

He nodded but didn't comment. He hated this—the uncertainty and not knowing where he stood. Had he messed things up so much before she left that they were going to go back to being just friends? The only thing he did know was that he wasn't willing to open that can of worms while they were in the car or in the grocery store. But the only way he was going to remain even partially sane was to get it out in the open once they were back at the cabin.

Of course they ran into half the town while in the grocery store and had to stop and talk to them. And once they were outside, it started to snow. While they were putting the groceries in the trunk, Melanie turned to him and smiled—a genuine smile. "Looks like we might get a white Christmas, huh?"

What? She was actually happy about something Christmas-related?

Josiah drove them to the cabin and did so in silence while Melanie told him all about the Christmas decorations and sites she had seen while in Manhattan. While he heard her talking, he couldn't help but wonder if he was somehow dreaming the whole thing. The woman who'd left only a few days ago was pretty anti-Christmas, while this one almost seemed to be looking forward to it.

By the time they had gotten home and unloaded the groceries and brought all of Melanie's things in, Josiah felt like he had to speak up.

"What in the world is going on here?" he snapped.

Melanie paused—she was in the middle of hanging up her coat when she turned and looked at him. "Excuse me?"

"You heard me. What's going on?"

"In regards to what?" she answered with a snap of her own. Shutting the closet door, she faced him and walked toward where he stood in the middle of the living room.

"You? Me? Us? Take your pick!"

Rather than answer him, she walked over and plugged in the Christmas tree, then sat down on the sofa where she looked up at him expectantly.

The last thing Josiah wanted to do was sit down. He'd been sitting in the damn car for hours between the trips back and forth to the airport and now he wanted answers! When he saw Melanie sitting there patiently, he sat down and faced her. "Well?"

"Well what?"

He growled in frustration and raked a hand through his hair before forcing himself to calm down. When he looked at her again, he noticed an amused look on her face.

And it seemed to break some of the tension.

"Okay, fine." Taking a steadying breath, he put it all out there for her. "I'm sorry for the way I reacted before you left. I got a little ahead of myself and started making plans for us when we'd never even seriously talked about the future. I had no right getting mad at you for not being able to read my mind."

"You got that right," she quipped softly and Josiah glared at her.

"Anyway, I'm sorry for the way I said things, but not for what I said," he began cautiously. "I love you, Mel. I know it's soon and we have some hurdles but that's never going to change. I fell in love with you right away."

"It was the naked in the tub thing," she teased. "You fell in lust."

He chuckled. "Okay, that first night it was lust, but as soon as we started spending time together, I knew. You're it for me." He paused. "I know it's soon and I know you need time and I promise not to push. I just…I just want to be with you, spend time with you, laugh with you, talk to you, all of it. And at the end of your three months, if you want to go back to Raleigh, then I'm okay with it. I mean, I'm not, but I will be." He gave her a lopsided grin. "Or I'll try to be."

She laughed lightly and shook her head as she looked at him. "I appreciate that."

"We can do the long-distance thing," he said quickly. "Lots of people do and…you know…I've never been to North Carolina so it might be fun to come and check it out."

"That could definitely be fun," she said noncommittally.

Something was off. One of the things Josiah loved about their relationship was the bantering they shared and right now this felt like a very one-sided conversation.

"Of course if you'd rather I didn't and you wanted a clean break, then…" he sighed and looked at her helplessly, "I'd really hate it. I'm not going to sit here and lie to you. I don't want you to go, but I understand that you have to. But if your leaving meant that this—what we have—is over? I…I…" His head dropped and his voice cracked.

Reaching over, Melanie put her hand over his. "Josiah?" she whispered. He looked up at her and knew everything he was feeling was written all over his face. "I didn't get to tell you about the rest of my trip."

He looked at her with confusion.

"I went to see my grandmother's attorney."

He felt like she had kicked him in the stomach. Was she trying to hurt him or was she just deliberately being mean?

With a sigh she said, "It turns out that I have a rather large dilemma on my hands."

"Why?" he asked almost belligerently.

"Well, it seems like there was more to my grandmother's request than I was originally told."

Silently, he waited her out.

"It seems that if I leave before the three months is up, the property won't be sold or given to a charity as I originally thought." She looked at him as if waiting for him to question her, but he didn't. "If I walk away before the end of the allocated time, *you* get the property."

"What?" he exclaimed. "How is that possible?"

She shrugged. "I think she was trying to do the right thing by both of us. On one hand she wanted to leave something to me—probably because of our weird history—but she also knew how much you wanted this property. By willing the property to me with the stipulation, maybe she was assuaging her guilt. We'll never know. But in my mind, this property always should have been yours." She sighed dramatically. "So that means I have no choice but to leave and go back to North Carolina. It's the only way to make sure the property goes to its rightful owner."

Josiah's head was spinning. Carol had given him the property, by possible default. He looked at Melanie. "I don't even know what to say."

"You want to know what I think you should say?"

The hint of sass in her tone told him he was going to like what she had to say, so he nodded.

"I think you should say, 'Melanie, you can go, but not until the day before the deadline and you need to go home and sell your house and come back here to me as soon as possible.' And then you should tell me you love me."

A slow smile spread across his face and he turned her hand in his and tugged her into his lap where he finally kissed her. "Anything else?"

She ran her fingers over his cheek, his jaw, his throat as she looked up at him. "Then you should probably remind me again why I'm going to love this whole Christmas thing you've been yammering about for weeks and then make love to me."

"Just to seal the deal?" he teased.

She shook her head. "No. Just because you love me."

Resting his forehead against hers, he considered his options until he finally said, "I don't think I can do any of that."

Melanie straightened and looked at him, her eyes wide with shock. "What? Why?"

"You've left out one very important detail and until it gets cleared up, we can't move forward."

Her brows furrowed as she tried to think about what she missed. "I…what did I forget?"

He smiled and did his best to look a little wounded. "You keep talking about how I love you but I've yet to hear you mention how you feel about me."

A small gasp escaped before she realized he was right. "Josiah Stone…I love you. Part of me keeps saying it's too soon to be true, but the rest of me knows there is no denying it." She cupped his face in her hands and kissed him softly on the lips. "I can't believe I could have missed this."

His dark eyes scanned her face. "Missed what, baby?"

"This. You. Us." She kissed him again. "If my father hadn't pushed me to come here and accept my grandmother's gift, then we never would have met." Tears filled her eyes as she said the words.

Josiah shook his head. "I would have found you," he whispered before pulling her close and kissing her deeply. Melanie melted into him and as he carefully maneuvered them until she was laying beneath him, he knew everything was going to be all right.

Chapter Eight

"There had better be a good reason why you're waking me up this early."

"It's Christmas morning! Don't you want to check and see if Santa came?"

One eye peered out from under the comforter. "You're kidding, right?"

Melanie bounced on the bed excitedly. "You have no one to blame but yourself! Now come on!"

Slowly Josiah rolled over and forced himself to sit up. "Mel, it's…" He looked over at the beside clock. "It's seven in the morning." Reaching for her, he did his best to convince her of all the reasons staying in bed would be better for them.

With a giggle, Melanie rolled away and stood up next to the bed. "You told me Christmas morning was like the best morning of the year," she argued playfully. "And being that you haven't lied to me about anything yet, I have no choice but to believe you. Now there is a mountain of presents out there that are just begging to be opened." She reached for one of his hands and tried to tug him out of the bed.

Laughing, he pulled it back and smiled when she landed on top of him. "It is the best morning of the year. This one in particular," he added before pulling her close and kissing her soundly. "Tell you what, give me another hour in bed with you and then the rest of the day is all yours. What do you say?"

Melanie looked as if she were considering her options when she quickly straddled him and pulled her nightie up and over her head.

A slow grin covered Josiah's face. "I'll take that as a yes."

****

Two hours later they walked hand in hand out to the living room and Melanie gasped with delight. "Oh my goodness! Look at this!" she cried. The tree was lit and there were presents everywhere—maybe even more than what had been there the night before. Her stocking was full and there was a fire roaring in the fireplace. "Boy, Santa is thorough."

"You know it," Josiah replied with a wink as he made his way to the kitchen. "I'm going to get us some coffee first."

With a small groan, she followed him and they worked together getting the coffee brewing. "You mentioned something about a special breakfast too."

He rolled his eyes. "You're a demanding little thing," he teased and gave her a loud smacking kiss on the cheek. "It's a good thing I love you."

Within minutes they were out in the living room and sitting on the floor. "Okay, I have to admit that I have no idea what we're supposed to do here," she confessed. "Do we trade off like I give you a gift to open and then you give me one?"

Standing, Josiah pulled her stocking off of the mantle and handed it to her. "You're supposed to see what Santa left for you first," he said and sat down beside her.

"Oooh…let's see…" she began and then marveled at the gifts. There was candy and a new pair of gloves and some other silly trinkets made her giggle. "I can't believe Santa brought mc ink for my printer."

"It can't all be about fun and games, Mel," he chuckled. "Santa is all about the practical sometimes."

"Duly noted," she said and when she finished going through the stocking, she looked over at Josiah. "Can I give you a present now?"

Josiah skimmed a hand over her cheek and all the love he felt for her shone in his eyes. "Sweetheart, you are the best present I ever could have received. I don't need anything else."

She gave him a wicked smile as she reached under the tree and pulled out his first wrapped gift.

"What the…"Josiah said as he opened the box. "An iPod? But…" He pulled it out of the box and immediately began to read the instructions.

"I thought it was time for you to retire your CD collection and join this millennium."

"Very funny," he said. "And very thoughtful. Thank you."

"It's already loaded with about two dozen albums. I raided your CDs to see what I should start with."

"You know you're going to have to show me how to use this, right?"

She nodded. "Not a problem." When she crawled toward the tree, Josiah's hand on her calf stopped her. "What?"

"What are you doing?"

"I was just getting more of your gifts to give you. I thought it would be easier since Santa seemed to scatter them around the tree and mixed them up with the rest of the presents." She pulled three boxes out and handed them to him.

"It's not my turn," he said playfully.

"Technically I already opened a few, if you count the stocking, so humor me and open these."

He grumbled about how this was not proper Christmas morning protocol, but he opened the presents anyway. He looked like a big kid as he unwrapped a pair of high-tech, wireless headphones, a Kindle and a watch.

"Mel," he began and sounded a little like he was chastising her, "you didn't need to do all of this."

"But I wanted to," she said simply.

Rather than argue, Josiah began pulling presents out from under the tree. Melanie watched curiously because he seemed to have some sort of order that he wanted to give them to her in. After several minutes, he sat back and sighed. "Change of plans," he said. "You have to open all of these gifts before I open another one. No arguing."

For some reason, she could tell this was important to him so she nodded. "Okay."

He handed her the first box. It was large and a little awkward and her curiosity was definitely piqued. As she pulled the wrapping away, she gasped and then looked at him in confusion. "I don't…I don't understand."

"Finish taking the paper off," he said softly.

She did as he suggested and it took a solid minute before she realized what she was looking at. "Oh my gosh," she whispered and looked up at him. "I wanted this doll so much when I was little! I can't believe you found this!"

"There are a lot of dolls out there," he said, grinning. "I had no idea how many there actually were."

"This is incredibly sweet," she said. "This was…this was the doll my mom was supposed to be getting for me…"

"I know," he said solemnly. "I know it's a little late but…"

Crawling over to him, Melanie kissed him. "I don't even know what to say."

Josiah positioned her so she was sitting back in her original spot. "You say 'What's next?' and then I hand you this." He put another large box in her lap.

Melanie quickly tore it open. "Roller skates?" she chuckled. "I haven't skated in years!"

"You did great when we went ice skating," he reminded her.

"I wish I could go outside and try these out right now!"

Josiah took the box from her lap and handed her another. For the next hour she opened up gifts that represented every year of her childhood that she didn't celebrate Christmas and he watched the joy and wonder on her face as she opened each and every one. And with each gift, she shared a memory as to why she had wanted it as a child. When she was done, her tears openly flowed.

"How…how did you do it?" she asked softly.

"I'd like to take all the credit, but I can't. The idea was mine but your dad filled in the gift suggestions. He has an amazing memory."

She nodded and then quickly looked around.

"What?" he asked. "What are you looking for?"

"My phone! I need to call him and tell him about all of this!" Jumping to her feet, she began to walk toward the kitchen.

"Mel, maybe you should wait."

"What? I really want to talk to him and…and…"

There was a knock at the front door that distracted her from what she was saying. She walked over and shrieked with joy when she opened the door. There on her doorstep, stood her father!

"Merry Christmas, sweetheart!" he said, wrapping her in his embrace.

"I can't believe you're here! I was just about to call you and…"

Josiah came up behind her and ushered them both away from the door and back into the house. "It's too cold out there to stand in the doorway. Can I get you a cup of coffee, John?"

"That would be nice. Thank you," John replied.

"I don't understand," Melanie said. "How…when did you get here?"

"I got in late last night."

"Why didn't you come here? Who picked you up from the airport? Or did you drive? I can't believe you didn't tell me you were coming!"

John laughed and hugged her close again. "I drove because the tickets were too expensive and it was worth the long hours to get here. I stayed at Josiah's last night and we planned this so I could be here with you this morning."

"But…"

Just then Josiah walked over and handed John a mug of coffee. "I texted him while you were in the bathroom and told him to give us an hour before coming over. I knew he got in late and wanted him to have the chance to sleep in."

"So that's why you distracted me this morning when I…" she stopped and blushed. "Never mind."

Josiah chuckled because he knew what she was referring to. "Yes. That's why I did it," he said. "Now let's go back inside and open more presents."

Melanie stopped and let out a soft cry. "I don't have anything here for you," she said to her father. "I mailed it up last week!"

John reached over and kissed the top of her head. "And I got it and I love it. Besides, this Christmas is all about you. So show me what Santa—and Josiah—got for you."

Together the three of them sat back down around the tree and talked about the gifts and Melanie's childhood memories. There were more presents under the tree—Josiah had made sure there were gifts for John too—and it was almost noon by the time they were done.

"I want the two of you to sit and relax and I'm going to go make us all some breakfast," Josiah said as he rose to his feet.

"It's a little late for that, son, don't you think?" John asked.

"We'll call it brunch," he replied, smiling. "We're under no schedules here today so we'll eat now and make dinner whenever we feel like it. How does that sound?"

"Perfect," John said.

Melanie stood and wrapped her arms around Josiah and raked her hands up into his hair as she smiled up at him. "Thank you."

"For what?"

She shook her head and chuckled softly. "Everything. You gave me so much here today and I feel like the luckiest girl in the world."

"That's good because being with you has me feeling the exact same way."

"Like the luckiest girl in the world?" she teased.

He kissed her soundly and when he raised his head, he whispered for only her ears, "When your dad leaves later, I'll prove to you what a lucky man I am."

Epilogue

Josiah couldn't help the anticipation he was feeling. Melanie was coming back from North Carolina today and if he timed it right, he was going to be arriving back at the cabin around the same time she was.

She was coming home.

To Silver Bell Falls.

Yeah, that made him grin like a loon and it felt great.

He turned onto the winding driveway that led to the cabin and felt like his heart was going to beat right out of his chest when he saw Melanie's car in the driveway with the U-Haul trailer behind it.

Two months ago she had told him she loved him and the simple fact that she was here just proved it all the more. After Christmas she had put her house in Raleigh up for sale and her father had handled most of the arrangements for it. And then, true to her word, she left Silver Bell Falls and contacted her grandmother's attorney to get the land signed over to him. Being that he planned on the two of them getting married, it was almost a moot point.

The property would be theirs together no matter what.

Pulling up beside her, he quickly rounded the car and gathered her up in his arms and spun her around before kissing her like he was a dying man and she was a feast. Luckily she seemed to feel the same way as him and before he knew it, he had her backed against the trailer ready to give the world a show!

Whispering his name between kisses, Melanie finally pulled away a bit. "I missed you so much," she said breathlessly.

"It was too long. Too damn long." And then he was kissing her again.

Melanie put a hand on his chest and gently pushed him away. "It was only ten days."

"Ten of the longest days of my life." He was breathless and turned on and he wanted nothing more than to take her inside and make love to her, but he could tell she had something on her mind. "What's going on, Mel? Is everything all right."

She chewed nervously on her bottom lip as she reached into her coat pocket and pulled out an envelope.

"What is it?" he asked.

"I got it yesterday before I got on the road. It's from my grandmother."

Josiah looked at her like she was crazy. "How...how is that even possible?"

"She wrote it before she died—at the same time she wrote her will. Her attorney sent it to me."

"Have you read it yet?"

She shook her head. "I'm a little afraid to."

Pulling her close, he hugged her and placed a kiss on the top of her head. "It's okay. You'll read it when you're ready." He let out a breath and did some mental calculations. "Tell you what, it's starting to get dark out so why don't we move as much of this stuff as we can into the cabin and then we'll have some dinner. What do you think?"

"Please tell me we're going to get some takeout!" she chuckled. "There's no way I am up to cooking anything tonight."

"Don't you worry," he said, kissing her again simply because he couldn't help himself. "It's already cooking and it should be done by the time we're ready."

She looked up at him in surprise. "You cooked dinner? Really?"

He tickled her ribs until she cried uncle. "Don't sound so surprised! I've cooked dinner for us plenty of times. It's nothing fancy, just some crockpot chili, but it will do."

"Oooh…I love crockpot chili. Thank you." She smiled up at him and then walked over to the back of the trailer and unlocked it. "You ready?"

He nodded.

Three hours later the trailer was empty, dinner was done and they were seated on the couch in front of a roaring fire.

"Welcome home, Melanie," he said softly, his arm around her, his head resting on top of hers.

Beside him, Melanie sighed. "It's good to be home."

****

It was two in the morning and Melanie couldn't sleep. Beside her, Josiah was sound asleep. Carefully, she rose from the bed and put on her robe before tiptoeing out to the living room. Everything was dark and the fire had long since gone out. With her heart hammering in her chest, Melanie walked over to the front closet and reached into her coat pocket and pulled out the envelope that had her grandmother's letter in it.

Slowly, she walked over to the sofa, turned on the small lamp beside it and opened the envelope. She took a steadying breath. "You can do this," she sighed and began to read.

To my dear Melanie,

I am sure this letter is a bit of surprise for you. After all, I didn't reach out to you while I was alive, so why would you expect a letter once I was gone? I want you to know how sorry I am. Sorry that I was prideful. Sorry that I was spiteful. And most of all, I'm sorry that I wasn't there for you like I should have been. I let the disagreement with your father affect our relationship and that never should have happened. You were an innocent victim in the whole thing and I wish there were a way to go back and change that.

If you're getting this letter, it's because you declined the property in Silver Bell Falls. I really wish you would have reconsidered. It's a truly amazing place. Some of the greatest memories of my life have to do with taking your father there when he was a child. There's nothing quite like a Christmas in Silver Bell. I had many friends there and I had always hoped that someday those friends would be your friends too. Maybe they'd be able to tell you about a side of your old grandmother that you didn't know existed.

And maybe you'd see that I wasn't such a cold-hearted person.

I made many mistakes in my life, Melanie, and it's a hard thing when you come to the end of your life and realize all of them and know that there isn't enough time to make them right. My hope was that you'd go to Silver Bell. The sheriff there, Josiah Stone, is an amazing young man. When I got to know him, in the back of my mind I imagined him being the kind of man who would make a good husband for you.

You see, you may think that I didn't know you, but I did. I always kept track of where you were and what you were doing. That probably makes me more of a coward since I didn't come and see you for myself. I won't make any excuses to you—I was wrong and I know it. I just want you to know that I am very proud of the woman you grew up to be and if time had allowed it, I would have told this all to you in person. But my time is coming to an end. I always thought there'd be more of it—time, opportunities. I was wrong about that and so many things. I hope that someday you'll be able to forgive me and think of me with a little less anger and maybe even a little understanding.

I wish you nothing but love and happiness, my dear granddaughter. And should you ever need a place to call home, I hope you'll consider going to Silver Bell.

All my love, Grandma

Tears were streaming down Melanie's cheeks. She re-read the letter another three times. When she looked up, Josiah was standing in front of the sofa looking sleepy and rumpled and so damn good to her that all she could do was stand up and wrap her arms around him.

"Are you okay?" he asked quietly.

She shook her head. "I finally read her letter."

He didn't say a word. He just held her.

She cried as if her heart were broken, and in a lot of ways, it was. Melanie lost track of time and when she finally lifted her head and looked up at Josiah, he cupped her face and used his thumbs to wipe away some of her tears.

"Do you want to talk about it?"

Rather than answer, she picked up the letter and handed it to him. They sat down on the sofa and snuggled together as he read it. When he was done, he let out a low chuckle. "Son of a gun," he murmured.

"She was trying to set us up," Melanie said.

He nodded. "She never even told me she had a granddaughter." He paused. "I'm not saying that to make you feel bad, it's just…"

"It's okay," she interrupted. "It's not important. Not anymore."

For a long time, he just sat there and held her. "I wish I knew what to say."

"Just tell me you love me."

"You know I do," he said, his voice barely a whisper.

She knew he was tired. She was too. Slowly, she disengaged from his arms and stood up, holding out a hand to him. "Come on. Let's go back to bed."

He stood with her hand in his, but he didn't move. When she looked up at him questioningly, he said, "I'm thankful for her. I know you may not want to hear that, but I am. You're here with me now and she had a hand in that so for that fact alone, I'll always be thankful to her."

Melanie gave him a small smile. "Believe it or not, I am too."

"Welcome home, Melanie," he said and drew her back into his arms.

"It's good to be back in Silver Bell with you," she replied and with a soft kiss, she led him back to bed.

####

Made in the USA
San Bernardino, CA
28 October 2015